CW00429926

Copyright

The Unsound Sister
By Lelita Baldock

ISBN: 9798558321203 (Amazon Paperback Edition)

Disclaimer
The characters in this book are entirely fictional. Any resemblance to actual persons living or dead is entirely coincidental.

Editing by Lucy Skoulding - Starlight Editing
Cover Art by Ryan Hewitt

First published November 2020
Visit: lelitabaldock.com

Thank you

The core idea for *The Unsound Sister* originated in 2014. Back then it was a just vague idea of two sisters and the question of guilt. Years later, when I took a trip to South Devon in the UK, I found the perfect location for the crime novel that had been developing in my mind ever since.

But having a basic plot and setting was not enough. Unlike my first novel, *Widow's Lace*, which required historical research, *The Unsound Sister* is a crime story. It depends heavily on the law and legal process.

I cannot say thank you enough to my father, Trevor Baldock, and his partner, Sharon Tonkes, for the *hours* of time they gave to me, sharing their years of legal experience. Without their guidance and, dare I say it, counsel, *The Unsound Sister* would never have eventuated. So to dad and Sharon, truly, thank you.

I also want to thank my unfailingly supportive husband for the cups of coffee and constant words of encouragement over the long hours of writing and editing this work.

To my brother Rick who always has my back, my beautiful mumma, Cynthia, and my dear friends who read the beta draft and took the time to give me honest and helpful feedback, you guys rock!

To my editor, Lucy Skoulding of Starlight Editing, you are incredible. Thank you for working with me on the final draft of *The Unsound Sister*. I have learnt so much from working with you, and I cannot wait to do it all again soon!

And finally to everyone who picks up *The Unsound Sister* and gives it a read - thank you for giving an independent author a chance. I truly hope you enjoy!

November

1: Beesands Hotel

How do you prepare yourself to meet a killer?

Damning headlines had been splashed across the morning papers for weeks: 'The Devil of Devon'; 'Spouse Slayer'; 'Husband Slasher - the baby was next!' Then, as further facts emerged: 'Time to talk: the death penalty in Britain'; 'Mental health in England: a new crisis or age old problem?'; 'The mind of a killer: fact and fiction in the Lane-Huxley case.'

She'd have to clamp down on that. Damn the media in this country. How could you get a fair trial when the jury already agreed with some article from the tabloids?

Harriet adjusted her rearview mirror, checked the mascara framing her hazel eyes, re-applied her lipstick and smacked her lips. Stepping from her Mazda, the spectre of St Bernard's Psychiatric ward loomed above her, its brown walls blending into the gloom of the overcast November skies. Nervously, she ran a hand through her long dark hair, then swept her hands down the front of her dark grey suit jacket and squared her shoulders.

'Chin up Harrie,' she whispered to herself and began the walk to reception.

Mason Simons raced into the dining room of the Beesands Hotel, menus in hand. She was late again, and Janet was on the war path. Didn't she understand it was hard to make it through traffic from art school? There was no compromise with Janet.

'Stupid,' she grumbled to herself.

Mason knew few guests would venture out on an out-of-season Thursday, especially one as grey and threatening as this. The guests upstairs would, of course, need feeding, but there were only three of them.

Hopefully Mr Huxley would dine in the restaurant, Mason smiled secretly to herself. The dark-haired businessman from London was really rather charming. 'Have you done the menus yet Mason?' Janet called from the bar.

Pulled from her dreaming, Mason sighed. 'Almost done,' she called and began to place the menus on the window tables. Light from the pale sun slanted into the dining room, the golden ball already almost dipping into the sea before her.

Movement caught her eye. Striding purposefully from the neighbouring pasture came a small figure dressed in jeans and a black jacket, golden buttons on the cuffs catching the sun. Mason raised a hand to wave to Eloise Lane-Huxley, Mr Huxley's wife, but she didn't turn towards the hotel, instead continuing on, at pace, eyes focused on the path before her. Even in the half light of impending sunset it was impossible to miss her beauty, she really was a ridiculously attractive woman. Jealousy speared through Mason. She shook it off, placed her last menu on a table and went to collect the candles.

Later, after Mason had settled the sole couple who had ventured in for a meal in a seat by the window, Janet placed a tray of soup and crusty bread before her. 'For Mrs Dalesford, in number 24.' Mason nodded taking up the tray and carefully mounting the creaky stairs. She traversed the dim hallway cautiously, the soup bowl was filled to the brim, potato and leek sliding thickly up the bowl's rim. Mrs Dalesford had sent Mason back for spilled soup before. Light shone from a doorway ahead. Not Mrs Dalesford's room, but Mr Huxley's. Mason eyed the shaft of light that spilled from the open door. She hadn't seen him leave, he must be inside, thinking himself concealed. Perhaps the door had bounced when he pushed it shut? The doors, like almost everything in this old building, were sinking into the carpets. Mason paused by the crack in the door.

'Mr Huxley?' she called, hoping to catch his attention. No reply, perhaps he was out after all.

'Mr Huxley?' she pushed the door with her elbow taking a step across the threshold. The soup, bread and bowl crashed to the floor. Mason screamed.

'Jesus. Fuck!' Detective Superintendent Robert Fields swore. Robert ran a hand through his salt and pepper hair, dark eyes assessing, tanned skin paling. He'd seen his fair share of murder scenes in his time, but this…

'Get the cordon up Jessie. No one in or out until we've cleared them.'

'Yes boss,' Jessie rushed away.

'Hotel staffer found him just after 6 p.m.,' Detective Inspector Anita Shan was speaking, pen poised purposefully over her notepad, 'She was taking room service to the old lady in room 24, just down the hall. Saw the door was ajar…'

'And walked into this.' Robert grimaced.

He stepped through the doorway, entering the room. The blood was everywhere, splashed up the walls, across the light carpeted floor.

That'll need redoing, Robert thought to himself from some disconnected part of his brain.

The body: male, caucasian, dark hair, was splayed out in the centre of the room, blood pooled beside his head. Kneeling a careful distance from the victim, Robert began his assessment.

'Cuts on his hands.' He indicated deep gouges along the victims palms.

'Defence wounds?' Anita supplied.

'I would guess so. Hard to tell right now, but looks like multiple stab wounds across his chest and stomach. But the neck…' Robert motioned to a jagged gaping wound across the throat, 'that probably finished him off.'

Anita blew out a breath. 'He's not a small man,' she observed.

Robert nodded absently, standing back up. Experienced eyes scanned the walls, the splatter over the dresser and cream bed duvet.

'Frenzied. Enraged. This wasn't some calculated killing. This was impassioned. Impulsive.'

'DS Fields,' a timid voice sounded from the doorway. The bobbie, David Hall, first on the scene hung back in the hallway. 'I just spoke with the hotel worker who found him, Miss Simons. Says his name is Grant Huxley. He is here most weekends, or at least has been since September.'

'Just the weekends?' Robert enquired.

'Yes, sir. He comes to visit his wife and kid. They live just up the coast in Torcross.'

'Do you have an address?'

'Yes, they live on Hiddley Drive.'

Robert and Anita's eyes met across the room. 'David, get a squad car to that house in Torcross. Now!'

Margaret Ives put down her home phone with a click. It was always so good to talk to her sister. Ellen may be in a home already, but her mind was still sharp. She'd have to make the time to visit in the next few weeks. Take a taxi this time, her hips really couldn't abide the bus anymore.

Margaret groaned as she stood, her arthritis was playing up again. It was the wet weather, it always got into her joints. 'Better than any weather forecast,' Harold always said. Margaret allowed herself a moment of emotional indulgence, feeling the hurt at the memory of her late husband pulse sharply, if briefly. A good man. *Enough now*. She shook her head and waddled to her kitchen. Time for a cup of tea.

Margaret ate early these days, especially when the sun set so quickly. The gathering dark always readied her stomach for food. But a good cup of tea, that was for anytime. She filled the kettle, placed it on the hob and moved to the fridge for milk.

Bang! A loud crash echoed through the house. Margaret started, hand on her heart. She worked to slow her breathing, pausing a moment to allow her heart beat to settle and made her way into the front room. Her front louvre window was thrown open, curtains billowing in the strong storm winds.

'Silly girl,' she chided herself crossing the room, 'should have shut the window, the wind is fierce out there.'

She pulled back the yellowed curtain and reached out into the cold, wet night for the louvre handle. Just then she spied a figure walking through the rain. Dark jacket, hood up. For a moment Margaret felt fear, who was this strange person out in the storm? But the face turned towards the light of her window and Margaret caught a flash of Eloise Lane-Huxley's pretty face. Her neighbour. 'Another silly girl,' Margaret whispered as she waved to her neighbour, 'out in this storm. At least she didn't take the baby.'

Eloise's face turned away. She didn't return Margaret's wave. 'Probably couldn't see me through the rain,' Margaret mused to herself as she pressed the lock down on the louvre, securing it in place.

The rain was coming down hard now, filling the windscreen faster than the wipers could clear it, but PC Tracy Berry didn't slow her pace. She'd been on her way home for the evening when the call came through. *Incident in Beesands, all respond.* So she'd responded. Then, just as she was pulling into the coast, her radio fired again, *Hiddley Drive Torcross. Wife of victim*. She'd flung the car around.

The sat nav had her following a strip of land between the sea and the Slapton Ley, an inland lake. Wild waves whipped against the coast, pale in the light of her headlights. 'Turn right in 5 yards,' the calm voice of the sat nav instructed.

'You're the boss,' Tracy murmured as she veered away from the wild tide. Her heart was pumping, adrenaline coursing preemptively through her veins. Not enough facts to be properly prepared; enough facts to be concerned. Murdered man in Beesands. A husband. Estranged from his wife in some way. It was the wife's house Tracy was bearing down on at speed through the storm.

What would Tracy find at the house? A murdered woman? God forbid! An enraged killer? Or a mother enjoying microwave dinner and watching the evening news?

Tracy pulled into an empty driveway. Lights on inside indicated someone was home. She stepped from her car and made her way to the front door. The screaming of a child cut through the sound of the pelting rain. A sensor light flicked on, illuminating the front porch and the open front door. A red smear shaped like a hand print shone from the door jam.

Tracy tensed, taking out her baton, holding it ready. 'Hello? Mrs Huxley? I'm PC Tracy Berry of the Devon and Cornwall Police. Is anyone home?'

No reply. Just the screaming child. Tracy entered the home.

A hallway, red spots dotted sporadically down its centre. Tracy advanced down the hall, keeping clear of the blood. It led to an open kitchen and lounge area, several rooms connecting to the central space. A bloodied jacket lay flung over a central dining table. Tracy brought her shoulder to her mouth and radioed despatch, 'This is PC Tracy Berry on Hiddley Drive, Torcross. I have blood on the scene. Investigating now. Request back up.'

'Copy that, PC Berry. Back up dispatched.'

Tracy advanced into the open room. The screams of the child came from behind a door labelled 'Jacob' in wooden letters painted in bold primary colours. She paced carefully but quickly towards the cries, moving her solid northern frame with the agility of a much younger woman. She may be nearing retirement age, but she kept up her fitness routine. She entered what was clearly a nursery, calming baby blues and creams filling the room, brightly coloured mobiles dangling from the ceiling, plastic toys gathered into a box by the door. In a cot against the wall, red faced from screeching, stood a small child, covered in blood.

'No,' Tracy gasped, rushing to the child. He lifted two fat arms up to her, beseeching. Tracy gathered him in her arms, running her hands over his small, pudgy body, searching for wounds. Nothing. 'Thank fuck,' she whispered as she jiggled the child on her practiced ample hip, his screaming calmed.

'Ok pet, I gotta put you down now, ok? I gotta go find your mum.'

What was going on here? A double homicide? Murder suicide?

Gently Tracy placed the boy back in the crib, and made her way back into the lounge. Behind her, his sobbing started again. She blocked out his distressed cries, softer now, exhausted, and continued across the house.

In the new silence she could hear voices. Baton in hand she paced towards them.

'No, no, stop it, stop it.'

'Lou, calm down. Listen... listen to me!'

'Get off me. Get off me!'

'Lou, please, just stop.'

Tracy approached the doorway. Taking a deep breath she shoved the door open.

A bathroom, tiled in green, met her eyes. Two women, light haired, one tall, one average height stood before her. Their clothes were drenched in blood.

Tracy went into automatic, 'Stop what you're doing!' she stated firmly, 'I'm PC Tracy Berry of the South Devon Police. Hands where I can see them.' She held her baton aloft, legs wide, instinctively lowering her centre of gravity.

The women turned to her, eyes wide, startled. The one on the right held out her hands quickly, blood slick over them, 'No, no,' she said, breathless, 'this is not what it looks like.'

'Stay still!' Tracy said. 'Are you hurt?'

'No, we aren't hurt,' the woman replied.

'It's not our blood,' said the second. Her hands were moving before her, as though conducting an orchestra, two white birds in the harsh bathroom light, 'It's Grant's blood.'

She turned two big blue eyes to Tracy and smiled warmly. Tracy's stomach dropped. 'Don't move,' she repeated, before radioing in a status report.

'You can use the house phone,' the second woman began, moving forward.

'Lou stop,' the first woman went to grab the second. Tracy stepped back, 'I said stay still!' she cried, voice shrill.

'I'm just trying to help…'

Something clattered to the tiles between the women with metallic ring. Tracy glanced down. There between their feet lay a pair of long, sharp crafting scissors. The red of blood clinging to the blades.

'There you are,' the second woman exclaimed with glee. 'I've been looking for you.'

Her hands reached down for the scissors.

Tracy swung her baton.

2: The Lane Sisters

DS Robert Fields entered the interview room at Exeter Police Station, rolled his shoulders and surveyed the scene. This was the important part. Get a confession, case closed. He and Anita had been checking witness statements at Kingsbridge Station when the call came in. Murder at Beesands. They'd been close, the first detectives on the scene. Horrific. A man's life ended in the most brutal fashion. Now Robert wanted answers and he was going to get them.

June Lane, age 40, sat in a steel-framed chair beside Andrew Peters from legal aid. Her blonde hair awry, her eyes wide and wild. Great red stains marred her crisp white shirt. She held her hands clasped together on the table before her, fingers shaking, nails coated in dried blood. She'd be pretty, in normal circumstances. Perhaps a little tall for Robert's tastes, but comely. She looked up at Robert, mouth quivering. Robert stood a moment, centring himself then took his seat beside Anita.

He arranged his folder of notes before him and nodded to Anita. She nodded back, pressed record and performed the official interview introductions. Together they paused a moment, allowing the tension to build. Part of the show.

'Ms Lane,' Robert finally began, 'We want to ask you some questions about the events of tonight, the 15th of November 2018. Specifically, how you, your sister and a small boy came to be covered in blood.'

Anita took up the questioning, 'The blood is believed to be that of Mr Grant Huxley,' she slid a photograph of Grant's mutilated body across the table. 'Mr Huxley's body was found tonight at the Beesands Hotel. We'll have the DNA results by tomorrow to confirm, but it seems a likely connection.'

Glancing at the photograph, June drew a shocked breath, a

trembling hand flew to her mouth, eyes welling with tears. Robert paused, drawing out the silence. June lowered her hand to the table and swallowed hard.

Robert continued, 'We believe you know Mr Huxley?' He waited.

June nodded slowly, 'Yes,' her voice croaked, dry and strained. Robert poured her a cup of water and slid it across the table. She took it, tried a grateful smile, failed and drank.

Clearing her throat with a small cough, she continued, 'Yes, Grant is my sister's husband.'

'The father of the child at the house?'

'Jacob, my nephew. He is Eloise and Grant's son.'

'As you can see from the picture, Mr Huxley is dead.'

June pressed her eyes together tight. Her shoulders bunched in, shrinking down towards the table.

'Can you tell me, Ms Lane, how you came to be covered in blood?'

June drew a shuddering breath, eyes fixed on the table, 'I thought she was hurt. I thought Jacob...' a sob caught in her throat. She broke off, tears streaming down her face.

'Take your time, Ms Lane,' Anita said. They sat patiently. June took another drink of water, two hands to steady the shaking cup. She gulped the liquid down noisily.

'I came home and there was blood... and then I found Eloise in the nursery with Jacob. I thought they'd been attacked...'

'Back up, Ms Lane,' Robert interrupted gently. 'Go back to the beginning. Where were you before you returned home and found your sister? Where were you between 5 p.m. and 6 p.m. tonight?'

June's eyes flicked up to his and back down again. 'I...,' she gulped, eyes scanning the table before her, 'I was in Salcombe. My car needed servicing. I dropped it at the garage. Benny's Garage.'

'At what time did you drop the car at Benny's?'

'Around 4:30 p.m., I think... then I caught the bus back to Torcross.'

'Go on.'

'I read on the bus, watched the sunset. Then I walked home. It was raining. I was annoyed that I hadn't brought my jacket. Then,' she paused, 'I saw blood, like a smear from a hand, on the door frame.'

She stopped, gripping her hands before her, breath coming in shallow bursts.

'Please continue Ms Lane,' Robert said.

'The door was ajar. I went inside, saw Eloise's jacket on the table, covered in red. Ooooh,' she let out a trembling breath, her breathing becoming more ragged. 'I called for Eloise. But she didn't answer. I ran to the nursery, thinking of Jacob. And there she was....'

'What was your sister doing, Ms Lane?' Anita prompted.

'Singing,' she looked up at Anita, eyes confused. 'She was singing to Jacob. He was laying in her arms as she rocked him gently, like she was putting him to bed, or comforting him.'

'You don't believe the child was in danger?'

'I... no, no Eloise would never hurt Jacob!' Her face crumpled into tears, 'She'd never hurt anyone...'

Robert and Anita waited. June gathered herself and continued, 'It looked so normal, just like any night except... except she was covered in blood. Jacob too. I ran into the room and grabbed Jacob, checked him over. But he was fine, no wounds. I put him down in his crib. He started to cry. I went to Eloise. Ran my hands over her, she seemed fine too. But there was so much blood.' She broke off looking down at her hands, at the dried blood still under her nails. 'I looked into her eyes, Lou's eyes. I asked her what had happened. She just stared at me blankly, like she wasn't even there. Her eyes... I've never seen her look like that before. I pulled her to me, hugged her. I was terrified, confused. Then Lou started screaming...'

'Lou is Eloise?'

'Yes, sorry, it's a childhood nickname.'

Robert nodded, 'Why did she scream?'

'I... I think the blood. I think she finally saw it. I asked her again what happened and she looked at me in horror, started putting her hands all over me. Asking *me* what was wrong... She thought I was hurt... I, I didn't know what was going on. You have to understand,' June leaned forward, eyes pleading. 'I thought something had happened to Eloise. I never thought...'

'What happened next?' Anita cut in, voice calm.

June continued, 'I took her to the bathroom. She was hysterical. Screaming, crying. Jacob was too. He wanted to be held, he was scared. I had to calm her down, so I took her for a shower. To wash her off, to see if there were wounds I hadn't found. I never thought... Then the police woman arrived.'

'For the tape, PC Berry is the police officer in question. She entered the premises at, 'Anita consulted her notes, '6:37 p.m. She called for back up after seeing blood on the front door.'

June nodded, 'Yes, she came in. Told us to freeze or stop or something. And the scissors... they fell on the floor. And Lou reached for them. I tried to stop her. Then the police woman hit her over the head and Lou collapsed.'

'PC Berry believed Eloise was going for the weapon. It was self-defence,' Anita said, tone hard.

June held up her hands in placation, 'Yes, yes, absolutely. I didn't mean...'

'Were these the scissors?' Robert cut in, sliding an image of a pair of long bladed crafting scissors across the table. The murder weapon.

June glanced at the blood-covered blades and looked away. 'Yes,' she said, voice small.

'And do you know who these scissors belong to?'

A pause, 'Yes,' another pause. The detectives waited. 'They are Eloise's crafting scissors.'

Robert felt a little flutter of excitement. It was all falling into place exactly as he had suspected. He worked to keep his face neutral, to not give away his eagerness to wrap up her evidence in a neat package for the DPP.

'So how did they come to be on the floor of the bathroom?'

'I don't know. They must have been in Eloise's pocket... then fell out when we were surprised by the police woman.'

'But you didn't notice them when you checked your sister for wounds in the nursery?' Anita asked. Robert shot her a look, eyebrows raised. *Good point*, he thought to himself.

'I...' June paused, eyes scanning. 'I, no I didn't. I guess I was just checking her chest... where the blood was.'

It was time. Robert leaned forward, 'Ms Lane, June, can you think of a reason why your sister would murder her husband?'

June let out a small startled cry. 'Oh, I don't think...'

'Look at the facts. We have a dead body, covered in stab wounds. And his wife was found covered in blood, in possession of a pair of bloody scissors. Now, we haven't got the forensics back yet, but I am willing to bet that the blood on you, on your sister and on these scissors is that of Grant Huxley. By your testimony, you were on the bus from Salcombe at the time of Mr Huxley's murder. Which only leaves one other possibility.'

'Eloise? Killing Grant? But why? No, I can't imagine... she is so gentle. A mother. She loves Jacob. No, no... This just doesn't make sense!'

'From where we are sitting we can't think of any other explanation. But the *why* is an interesting question. Can you tell me why Mr Huxley was staying at the Beesand's Hotel and not with you and Eloise in Torcross?'

June stared at him, eyes wide. Slowly realisation dawned across her face, making her face look tired and drawn. She knew, he knew, 'They were estranged. Grant left Eloise after Jacob was born.'

'Go on.'

A battle took place across June's features, finally she slumped, defeated. 'Eloise hasn't been herself, 'she began. 'After Jacob was born she suffered from severe post-natal depression. When Grant left we brought her to Torcross for the calm, to help her recovery. I moved in to help out.'

'And Mr Huxley?'

'About two months ago he started visiting. We thought he wanted to reconcile, but…'

'But?'

June sighed heavily, 'A letter came this week, from the Family Court. He was applying for sole custody of Jacob.'

Boom!

Robert and Anita glanced at each other. And so it all clicked into place. Weapon. Opportunity. Motive. The final piece of the puzzle.

'But, Lou didn't know that!' June said urgently. 'I kept the letter from her. She'd been doing so well lately and I knew this would set her back. So I hid it. She didn't know.'

'And you don't think she may have found the letter? Applying for custody while working on a reconciliation could very easily seem like a betrayal…'

'Please,' June said, 'I don't know. But Eloise, she isn't a murderer. She is soft and sweet and forgetful… this, this just isn't her.' She looked up at Robert, eyes pleading. He felt his heart give at the mix of pain and hope he saw there.

'Thank you for your time, Ms Lane,' Robert said, 'I think we'll leave it there for now.'

Robert sat at his desk in Exeter, paperwork in piles around him. He really did have some serious organising to do, but not yet. First he had to deal with Eloise Lane-Huxley. He glanced at the clock. Fuck it had been a long night.

'How's it going boss?' Anita said, leaning against his desk and placing a fresh cup of coffee before him.

Robert rubbed his face, trying to work some life back into his skin and smiled gratefully up at Anita. Her dark eyes looked worn, tendrils of her hair escaping her neat ponytail. Still, she looked like she could keep working for another shift... he knew he looked far the worse.

'Still not talking?' he asked.

'Oh she's talking,' Anita rolled her large eyes. 'Talking isn't the problem. It's saying anything that makes sense. Lawyers making noises about her mental state. Saying we should pause the interviews. That she is not fit to answer questions.'

'So stop. We can't risk it. Any evidence she gives could be clouded by her state of mind. A good defence would get it thrown out of court.'

'Already done. She's in holding, having a cup of tea and a break.'

Robert shook his head ruefully. Eloise Lane-Huxley was a difficult culprit. So blonde and lithe and elegant. Pretty. Covered in blood. No memory of the night before or how she came to be in possession of a possible murder weapon. He usually did well interviewing the female suspects, they liked his face he suspected, came to trust him. And he knew how to use that connection to his advantage. The sister, June, had fallen straight into his charm offensive. But Eloise Lane-Huxley....

'Do we believe her, or is she faking?' he asked Anita.

'Hard to tell... but she does seem genuinely confused.'

Robert nodded, musing. Young mothers were hard to picture as murderers. It would be a tough sell to the jury. Their case would have to be solid.

'Ok,' he said, 'we still have six hours of holding before we have to let her go. Or charge her. So, have we got enough?'

Anita frowned, contemplating. She held up a finger, counting off. 'We have a potential murder weapon, the scissors that belonged to Eloise. We have a witness who saw her at Beesands at around 5:30 p.m., we have her neighbour seeing her return home around 6:20 p.m., in the rain.'

'So she was in Beesands at the time of Mr Huxley's murder. She was found covered in blood. Her sister says she and Mr Huxley were estranged, that he wanted the boy.'

'And she went mental when we showed her the custody letter.'

Robert nodded, eyebrows high. 'Yep, that was definitely unexpected.'

All interview Eloise had been calm, serene, like she didn't realise where she was or what she was being asked. She didn't even seem to understand that Mr Huxley was dead. But then they showed her a photocopy of the custody letter. She had read it silently, breathing becoming shallower and shallower, and then… she exploded. Face red with rage, eyes wide with anger. She had shouted incoherently. Arms flailing wildly. They had suspended the interview, let her calm down. Hours later when they resumed she was calm and detached again. They had shown her the letter a second time but she had just stared off into space, eyes glazed. No reaction. Like she was numb.

'What's your gut say?' Robert asked Anita.

'She and her sister were covered in blood. But June has an alibi,' she paused, 'Eloise did it, sir.'

Robert nodded, it was what his gut said too. June Lane had been a distraught but credible witness. He believed her.

'DS Fields?' a young officer walked into the office, 'this just came for you. From forensics.' He handed Robert an email print out.

'The blood results?' Robert asked hopefully, reaching for the page. His eyes scanned the results, his focus narrowed, his senses stilled.

'DI Shan, please get the DPP on the phone. We're going to charge Eloise Lane-Huxley with the murder of Grant Huxley, her husband.'

3: Swinging batons and coffee

The coffee cup tumbled. The dark brown liquid spilling over the side. PC Tracy Berry quickly licked the dribble from the side, scorching her tongue on the hot ceramic, but stopping the drip from falling onto her work shirt. She took a small slurp and returned the cup to its saucer. Placing her hands firmly on the table to steady the tremor she looked up sheepishly at DS Robert Fields.

His dark eyes watched her, shining with sympathy and his comforting smile was understanding. There was no trace of judgement or ridicule. He had a kind face, tired, lined by stress and time but still attractive. He had aged well.

'Sorry,' Tracy breathed, 'I'm just shaken up.'

Robert shook his head slowly, 'Nothing to apologise for. It's a natural reaction. I've been in this job 25 years and I nearly bottled it at the murder scene. It's an intense case.'

Tracy shrugged dismissively, 'I should be better at this by now. I've been back almost a year.'

'Takes time to get into the swing of it. This job is tough. We've all been there, don't beat yourself up about something we all experience.'

Tracy smiled thankfully. Joining the force had been a natural progression for Tracy; the daughter of a Sergeant, she became a bobbie, married an Inspector, took mat-leave and popped out three kids, then 15 years later divorced the (now) Chief Inspector and returned to the beat.

But Tracy didn't mind, the job had always called to her. Still, starting again at 55 did present a unique set of challenges. And seeing that baby...

The image of the small boy, plump from youth, tiny hands reaching, jumpsuit stained red with blood momentarily filled her vision. She shivered despite the warmth of the cafe.

'Thank you for this,' she said to Robert.

Robert nodded. Tracy had just been into his station to give her statement about the events of November 15th. She'd been first to the house on Hiddley, the one who found the Lane sisters. In the stress of the moment she'd believed herself to be under threat and had struck Eloise Lane-Huxley, with her baton. Fortunately, the suspect was fine, and just needed a few stitches. But they had to do due diligence. And Tracy was a witness. What she found when she arrived on the scene formed an important part of he and Anita's case against Eloise Lane-Huxley. Still suffering from memory loss (no link to Tracy's baton, thankfully confirmed), Robert and Anita had had to piece together the events themselves. No different to most cases really. Few murderers confessed the truth.

When Tracy had finished her story Robert had felt satisfied. Her testimony fit with June Lane's nicely, strengthening their case significantly. Eloise Lane-Huxley was the culprit.

Anita had thanked Tracy, telling her she could go. But Robert had seen it, that haunted look. Casually, as he walked her from the station, he suggested they grab a cuppa. Tracy had agreed, her face a picture of gratitude. Sometimes you needed to talk. Not just give evidence.

'You've nothing to worry about with the review,' he said. 'It is a clear case of self-defence. There was a weapon and Ms Lane-Huxley ignored your order to stay back. Open and shut.'

Tracy released a heavy sigh. 'That's good to know. When she reached for those scissors…'

Robert took a chance, reached forward and folded his hand about her own, squeezing lightly.

Tracy smiled, then frowned, eyes studying the wood grain of the table top. Robert waited, giving her the space to find what she wanted to say.

'It's the baby I can't get out of my head. The little boy. When I first saw him there I thought…' her throat constricted, choking off her words. 'He was just so small. I forget my boys were that tiny once…' she gave a short laugh. 'To think what might have happened if the sister hadn't got there when she did. What she was going to do to him. That innocent little boy.'

'There's no evidence that Eloise was going to hurt the boy, Tracy. Her sister testified that she was singing to him.'

Tracy glanced up at Robert, eyes hooded. 'Look what she did to her husband,' she paused. 'No sister wants to believe their sibling capable of murder, yet she did it. That boy was probably next. She still had the scissors on her.'

Robert squeezed her hand again and then let go, bringing his hands together before him. He understood Tracy's point of view. Arriving to a home in the dark, blood on the walls and floor and finding a screaming child covered in blood... It would be hard to step back and view it objectively, emotion was bound to be at play. Thankfully, Tracy had still been a good witness, recounting the events clearly and professionally. This coffee was for her to vent what was stirring within. She needed to talk it out. To release the burden of her experience by sharing it with someone else. Who better than a fellow cop? He knew from his own life the value of that connection, of feeling understood.

Robert just had to remember to keep to the facts himself.

He saw Tracy's argument. And with Eloise's mental state, could they be sure Jacob wasn't next?

But Robert had interviewed June Lane. He had seen the light of honesty in her eyes and didn't believe she was misrepresenting the events of the night. She'd found her sister singing Jacob to sleep, albeit covered in blood. No, Eloise's grievance was with her husband. Robert didn't believe she'd been a risk to the child. Even if the press were loving that particularly dark angle.

Regardless, June seemed a very practical and capable woman, a witness he could trust. Then again, so did Tracy...

He didn't say any of this of course, there was no need. Tracy would come to peace with the night in time, right now she just needed support. It would be a shame for the force to lose her because of the trauma of this horrid night. The community had lost enough.

'The boy is safe now,' he said instead. 'Family Services were contacted and have done their routine visit. They agreed he should remain in the home with his aunt. It's where he lived already and with close family, his everyday will be mostly the same. By their assessment he is happy and well, no residual trauma.'

'Good,' Tracy smiled weakly, 'children are very resilient aren't they?'

'They can be yes,' Robert said, though he cast his eyes aside. His years of service had shown him the lie in that belief. Children saw more, understood more than we liked to think.

'I think in Jacob's case he is simply too young to have understood any of what was happening,' he said, hoping it was true.

'Poor little pet. At least he has a loving family around him.'

'That he does.'

Tracy drained the last of her coffee, took a deep breath. 'I've taken up enough of your time DS Fields. But thank you. This,' she gestured vaguely around the cafe, 'this was really helpful.'

'We all need it sometimes,' Robert replied, 'a coffee and a chat, outside of the office.'

'Yeah,' Tracy said, 'I'll be sure to remember that myself.'

'And don't rush the healing process. It takes time to get over a situation like Hiddley Drive. Be kind to yourself, ok?'

'Ok, I'll try to remember that too.'

Robert saw Tracy to her car and watched as she pulled out into traffic, beginning the trek back to Salcombe. He hoped he'd been able to offer her some relief and comfort. At least the case should go smoothly, their evidence was strong. For once they'd got the killer off the streets almost immediately. It was nice to have one go right for a change. Didn't happen often in his profession. He'd take the easy win when he could. Slipping his hands into his jacket pocket, warming them against the brisk breeze of coming winter, Robert headed back to the office, his paperwork wasn't going to do itself.

4: The Devil of Devon

The Orchard, an interesting name. A place to grow fruit. A place to heal 'fruity' people. Odd choice of metaphor for the psychiatric ward of St Bernard's Hospital, Ealing, London. Housing a mere 20 'medium level' patients on its female wards; the worst offenders, murderers, murderesses. All with unstable minds. *The Orchard, sounds almost peaceful,* Harriet mused. It's reputation had nothing on the horror of Broadmoor, the men only facility famous for hosting some of Britain's most notorious and depraved minds: Peter Sutcliffe, the Yorkshire Ripper; serial killer, Robert Napper; Kenneth Erskine, the Stockwell Strangler. Yet as Harriet walked through the heavy entrance doors, she felt her stomach flip. Not infamous, true, but still a place of darkness. A worn looking nurse dressed in blue checked Harriet in, telling her she had to leave her purse and phone but could take her folder of case files, and led her down a long white corridor to the interview rooms.

'Wait here,' the woman, Betty, said, indicating a chair by an empty table. 'Ms Lane-Huxley's nurse, Amelia Warren, will bring her shortly.'

Harriet settled herself. Soon the door swung open and a younger, but equally fatigued nurse with brown bobbed hair walked in, Eloise in her custody. Harriet rose in greeting. Eloise did not look at Harriet, just floated past the table and took her seat. Amelia gave Harriet a small smile and took up a seat just to the side of lawyer and client.

Harriet sat back down across from Eloise Lane-Huxley, age 32, the *Devil of Devon*; husband murderer, her client. She sat motionless, large blue eyes fixed on the white table between them. Pale faced in a cream shirt and black trousers, shoulders pulled towards her centre. She was a diminutive woman, thin fair hair, pale skin, a smattering of freckles across the bridge of her nose. She didn't look like a woman who had been poised to kill her son, whatever the tabloids said.

Harriet cleared her throat. 'Mrs Lane-Huxley, my name is Harriet Bell. I am a solicitor from Healy Lawyers in Exeter. Your parents have hired me to defend you against the case being made by the DPP.'

She paused, waiting. Eloise showed no sign of having heard her, eyes still focused on the table.

'Have you everything you need here at The Orchard?'

Silence.

'Mrs Lane-Huxley, Eloise, I am here to talk to you about the events of November 15th 2018. The night your husband, Grant Huxley, was murdered. You have been accused of committing the crime.'

Still no response. 'I want to hear your account, in your own words. So I can begin preparations for the trial.'

Nothing.

'Eloise, do you understand what you are accused of?'

Blue eyes suddenly flicked up, pupils narrowing as they focused on Harriet. Surprise lit Eloise's face, as though she was noticing Harriet for the first time. 'Oh, forgive me. So rude,' she stammered. 'I didn't offer you tea. How do you take it? White? Sugar? Just a moment…'

She glanced around the room: clinical white walls, a single window overlooking the brown and cream exterior of the next wing, the fluorescent light's harsh beam washing everything in cold, sterile tones.

'I… oh,' her hands fluttered elegantly before her as she mimed placing a cup and saucer down, then pouring from a kettle. She paused, face ashen, hands shaking and looked up at Harriet. A little embarrassed smile passed across her lips and she brought her hands to her lap.

'So sorry, I… I sometimes, forget.' She indicated the space around them, shamefaced and settled her gaze on Harriet, eyes open and clear. Harriet paused a moment, careful to keep her face neutral. How could one forget being in The Orchard?

'Not a problem Mrs Lane-Huxley.'

'Call me Eloise.'

Harriet nodded, 'Eloise, can you talk me through the night of November 15th?'

Eloise swallowed, her throat bobbing nervously. 'You have the transcript? Of the interview?'

'I want to hear it in your words, Eloise. Take your time.'

Harriet sat, pen poised and waited patiently. Eloise shuffled in her seat, hands wringing on the table before her.

'Well, it was a Thursday. I usually go for a walk on Thursday and June minds Jacob for me. June is my sister, she lives with me. When I get home, she goes to our parents for dinner.'

'Every Thursday?'

'Yes, every Thursday. So I know I don't have to cook for two on Thursdays...' She paused, confusion flickering over her face.

Harriet prompted, 'Please go on.'

'So I planned to take a walk anyway, bundle Jacob up, take Bella, she's our dog. I love the sunsets. ... But it looked like rain, so I decided to skip it and work on my crafting instead.'

'Your crafting?'

'Oh yes,' her eyes lit up, 'I make all kinds of things. Scrapbooks, tableaux, picture frames... anything. I was working on a felt photo book for Jacob's 1st birthday... but I couldn't find my scissors. I looked everywhere... and then...'

She looked down at her small hands, they began to shake. Harriet waited in silence. 'And then June was screaming at me, pulling Jacob away from me and pushing me through the house, into the bathroom. I didn't understand, so I tried to get around her, back to Jacob, but she wrapped herself around me. She was shaking, trembling. I hugged her back. That's when I felt it. Sticky wetness. The blood. It was everywhere, all over June, all over me. My hands.' She paused, opening and closing her hands before her, palms up. Her eyes pressed closed as she worked through the memory.

'Then there was a woman, a large woman, standing in the doorway. I wanted to welcome her, but June stopped me. And then, there they were! My crafting scissors, on the bathroom floor. I went to pick them up and... everything went black.'

'The woman was PC Tracy Berry of the South Devon police. She thought you were a threat. She knocked you out with her baton.'

'Yes,' Eloise said quietly.

Harriet flicked through some pages before her, ostensibly checking her notes, but really just giving Eloise time to settle. 'Your sister gave evidence to the police that she had been in Salcombe dropping her car off to be fixed. She caught the bus home and found you in Jacob's bedroom, you and your son covered in blood.'

'Yes.' Eloise had gone even whiter.

'She says she ran to you, thinking you were hurt and dragged you into the bathroom. Then the police came and you dropped the scissors on the floor. You don't remember holding the scissors?'

'I, I don't remember anything but June screaming and then seeing the scissors on the floor.'

Harriet nodded, 'You know Mason Simons?'

'Yes, she works at the Beesands Hotel. Where Grant stays when he visits.'

'Miss Simons says she saw you walking along Beesands beach wall at around 5:30 p.m. that evening, watching the water. She was setting the dinner room, and the sky was darkening. But you say you skipped your walk because of the weather.'

'I, well, I mean, yes I planned to skip the walk...'

'Planned to?'

'I, I remember deciding not to go for a walk. But the police say I was seen in Beesands, so I must have changed my mind.'

'Could it have been someone else local? Not you?'

'Only my sister really looks like me...'

'But she was on a bus coming back from Salcombe.'

Eloise stared blankly at Harriet. 'But it was Thursday... she has dinner with mum and dad.' She broke off, looking flustered and confused.

Harriet tried a different tack, adding some detail from Mason's statement to see if it prompted a memory. 'Coming back to the walk. Miss Simons says you were alone. No dog or baby. Just you. She said you looked cold. She didn't see you leave, she was called away to work. So if you were there, on the beach, who was looking after Jacob?'

Eloise looked at Harriet, face stricken. 'I, I don't remember. I don't remember being there. I don't remember leaving Jacob, or walking to Beesands. I don't remember seeing Grant. I don't even know why he was there!'

'Pardon me? What do you mean, why he was there?'

'It was Thursday. Grant comes down after work on Fridays, stays until Sunday evening, so he can spend the weekend with Jacob and me. We are,' a swallow, 'we *were* working at getting back together.'

'So you didn't know he would be at the hotel that night?'

'No, I wouldn't have expected him until Friday.'

Harriet paused, scanning her notes. 'The blood report confirms the blood that was found on you and June, and the scissors, was that of Mr Huxley.'

Eloise gulped, eyes wide.

'Can you explain how the blood came to be on you, your sister and the scissors?'

'I... No, I just, I just don't remember. I hear what you are saying, that I was seen at Beesands, coming home. That the... blood, was Grant's. But, Ms Bell, I just don't understand. I don't remember being there. How could I walk all that way, how could I do that... how could I not remember?'

'That, Mrs Lane-Huxley, is what I aim to find out.'

The two women sat in silence a moment, each in their own thoughts.

'So, what happens now?' Eloise asked.

'Now we wait. The Prosecution is putting together its case. Once I have their evidence I can review and plan our case. For now we should consider Barristers to present your case in court. One I highly recommend is Randell Dawes QC. I can't guarantee he will be available, but his experience...' Harriet stopped, Eloise was no longer listening, her gaze had drifted back to the window, her body slumped forward.

'Eloise?' Harriet prompted.

There was no light of acknowledgement in Eloise's eyes. In fact, there was nothing in her eyes at all.

The young nurse came forward and placed her hands on Eloise's shoulders, moving to look into her patient's eyes. A small crease marred her brow.

Turning to Harriet she said, 'I'm sorry Ms Bell. She's having one of her turns.'

'Turns?'

Amelia blushed prettily. 'The wrong term, it's true. Eloise is prone to moments of amnesia. She blanks out for a while. It's mostly fleeting, like when you first arrived. But right now I think she's gone deeper. It seems to be related to stress... but we are still observing.'

'Right,' Harriet nodded. 'Well, I guess that's that then. When do you expect to have the preliminary report on her condition?'

'That I can't say. Doctor Taylor handles the complex cases. But as soon as the report is ready it will be sent through.'

Yeah, to the DPP. Harriet suppressed her aggravation. This young nurse was not responsible for the ways of lawyers, it wasn't professional to express frustration in front of her. Harriet would get to see that report, but it grated that the prosecution had first access, even if it just was the way of things.

'Well, I will leave you to her care. Thank you for your time, Ms Warren.'

The nurse nodded gently and turned her attention to Eloise. Harriet, gathering her documents, watched as Amelia helped Eloise to her feet, and, one arm about her shoulders, guided her towards the door. Eloise's pupils were large and dark, almost swallowing the blue of her irises, her face slack, arms loose at her sides. They passed Harriet.

'Until next time, Ms Lane-Huxley,' Harriet said.

Not even a flicker of reaction crossed her client's face.

'Good afternoon Ms Bell,' Amelia said.

Harriet followed them out of the door watching a moment longer as Eloise shuffled slowly down the long, brightly lit corridor.

She looked so fragile, so vulnerable. A sense of unease began to roil in her gut.

A murderer? She frowned and headed for reception to collect her things.

Walking out of The Orchard, Harriet mused to herself on just how oddly comfortable she'd felt when talking with Eloise. It definitely wasn't the case that she was comfortable in The Orchard itself. She'd been in her fair share of prisons to work with clients, so it wasn't the restrictions of the place, but something about the ward set her senses on high alert, despite the sober calm of the staff. No, she was comfortable with *Eloise*. Her warmth and open face. Harriet didn't know if she'd ever met someone who felt less like a devil in disguise. A strange murderer, educated, from a good family. Eloise really didn't fit the expected mould.

Shaking off the strange feeling that emanated from the back of her mind, straining to be acknowledged, she began the two hour drive back to Exeter.

December

5: *It's a family thing*

Harriet closed the door to her apartment on Denmark Road, Exeter. Kicking off her heels in the hallway she padded to the fridge on stockinged feet. Outside was the deep dark of winter nights, the chill of the air held at bay by the apartment's boiler. Harriet pulled a bottle of chardonnay from the fridge and stuffed two slices of bread into the toaster. Popping the top of the bottle she poured herself a generous glass before cracking open a tin of baked beans, pouring them into a bowl and microwaving them for two minutes. Leaning against the kitchen bench she took a long deep drink of the wine. The toast popped, the microwave beeped. Harriet assembled her beans on toast, and, wine bottle tucked in the crook of her arm, walked to the dining table against the wall. Pushing aside mounds of paperwork, folders and legal reference books, Harriet placed her plate on the table and sunk into a seat. Sipping from her wine she opened her laptop and began browsing through her emails. 53. *I take one afternoon out*, she thought. Harriet sighed and closed the laptop, leaning back in her chair. She'd deal with the backlog later.

For now all she could think about was Eloise Lane-Huxley.

Such a small woman, frail in fact. Those big blue eyes were heart breakers for sure. To think she had taken up a pair of crafting scissors and stabbed her husband to death, 14 times no less and slit his throat. *Crazy*. She seemed so, gentle.

The past weeks of working the case had only made the disconnect stronger. Something tugged at the edges of her mind, but she couldn't yet put her finger on it.

Frustrated after yet another meeting with Eloise had ended with her client's eyes staring off into oblivion, rather than returning to the office, Harriet had called up her uni friend Phoebe Giles and the two

29

had met for coffee on Market Street.

'I don't know Phebes, something just doesn't feel right,' Harriet lamented.

Phoebe had sipped from her coffee mug, eyeing Harriet over the rim. 'When did you last have a night out?'

Harriet scowled at her friend. 'Dancing doesn't fix everything Fi.'

Phoebe shrugged eloquently, smoothing her long dark hair over her shoulder, 'I was more thinking a good fuck… but however you want to dress it up.'

'You are the worst!' Harriet exclaimed, though she could not keep the smile from her face.

Phoebe was direct and blunt, and damn that could be refreshing.

'No time just now, Fi. And besides, men are overrated.'

'Don't need to tell me that,' Phoebe replied, grinning salaciously, a twinkle in her eye.

Harriet smiled, waving her hand to concede the point. Conversation shifted and swirled and cruised as the early dark settled around them. Kissing Phoebe on the cheek in farewell, Harriet had felt reset, tired, but lighter somehow.

It had been worth the email backlog to sneak in a few hours with her dearest friend. But as she walked the streets, illuminated by the glaring phone screens of passersby, her thoughts shifted, returning to the challenge before her.

Harriet shook her head and crunched into her beans on toast, chewing thoughtfully. Was the insanity defence the best route? Eloise was clearly not all there in the head, no memory of the event, forgetting she was in a mental hospital; who forgot they were on a psych ward?

But then other memories, like when Grant would visit and where her sister would be on a Thursday night were clear as day. It was a concern for her defence. So far the prosecution seemed willing to play ball on the insanity option. When the Magistrate refused Eloise's bail application, citing the heinous nature of her crime (Harriet couldn't really argue with that after seeing the pictures), the DPP had requested she be remanded in custody at The Orchard for psychiatric assessment pending trial. But would they change their mind as they investigated? Would Eloise's eloquence play against her? It certainly counted against the M'Naghten Rules; she had a full understanding of right and wrong.

Could there be a history of domestic violence to throw into the mix?

Grant and Eloise were separated at the time. He had left her after the birth of Jacob. Abandoned her while she was ill.

That she'd suffered greatly from post-natal depression was another tick for the insanity defence. But was Grant's neglect as a husband the more pertinent point?

Harriet reached for the wine bottle and topped up her glass. Perhaps she should consider the automatism angle; that Eloise's actions were not voluntary, some temporary disease of the mind, caused perhaps by the post-natal depression. There was no evidence that she was drugged, so the loss of control wasn't from an external source. Internal then, making the case a variant on the insanity plea. There had been a few recent cases in Exeter using just that approach. She'd have to read up on the details and outcomes...

Her mobile blared into life, interrupting her train of thought. Harriet snapped her hand across her desk and took up the blaring device. Call from: Home. She frowned. It had been a long day, all she wanted to do was sink into her wine and her case, not talk to Anne Bell. But, like a dutiful daughter, she pressed the green button, 'Hi mum, lovely to hear from you.'

'Harrie love, I'm glad I caught you. I tried earlier but you didn't pick up.'

Harriet rolled her eyes, glad her mum couldn't see her. 'I was at work, mum.'

'You are effectively self employed Harrie, you can take a call from your mother.'

'Not from inside St Bernards I can't.'

'St Bernards? What on earth were you doing there?'

'New client, can't say much else for now. So, what can I do for you?'

'Well, I am just checking in about Christmas. You were coming up on the Wednesday to stay the week?'

Harriet closed her eyes and squeezed the bridge of her nose. Sitting up straight, bracing herself, she replied, 'Yeah, about that. This new case... I won't be able to take that much time off. But I will still be there for Christmas lunch, that I promise.'

'Harrie, we haven't seen you since Easter. You need a holiday. Christmas is about family.'

Suppressing a sigh Harriet stretched her neck and replied, 'It's a big case mum. My first murder. I'll come up once it's done, stay a week. I promise. But Christmas, it's just right in the middle of the workload. But I will be up for the day. Ok?'

31

Her mother's sigh was heavy and frustrated. 'There's no point trying to change your mind Harrie, there never was. I'll tell Billy he can have his lady friend stay over, she can use the spare room.'

Harriet swallowed a laugh. Her brother William, Billy to his friends, Billy Bell (her parents really hadn't thought that one through) was 29 years old. Surely old enough to have his 'lady friend' stay in his room… But Harriet declined to argue. She'd got out of a week of family time, she wasn't going to push her luck by telling her mum how to run her good Catholic household.

'Would have been nice to have one of my girls for the night though,' her mother continued.

Harriet pressed her lips together tightly as Nellie's face swam up from her memory to fill her heart and mind. Her older sister. The one who got away first…

'How is Billy?' Harriet asked, shifting the topic.

'Oh, you know Billy, same old same old. Getting less shifts at the factory. All this Brexit talk is making your father nervous. But General Motors have assured them all the work will remain. Politicians, they just stir up trouble don't they? Threats. We were fine before the Union and we will be fine after it too.'

'And dad's heart scan went ok?'

'Yes, Fergus is just fine. I've had him on the DASH diet since that little scare in July. He grumbles about eating veal, calls it bloodless, but well, it's not up to him, is it?'

Harriet smiled to herself. Anne might call Harriet stubborn, but Harriet knew where she got it from.

'No mum, sounds like you have him under control.'

'That I do.'

'Look mum, I am sitting here staring at a pile of paperwork that's not going to do itself and I have an early start tomorrow. So I'm going to go. Give dad a hug for me and I will see you in a couple weeks. Ok?'

'Ok love, you take care. And if things change and you can stay a while, just say. I can have the room set for you in a jiffy.'

'Thanks mum. Love you, bye.'

Harriet hung up the phone and took another bite of her now cold beans and toast. The paperwork was real, but it wasn't getting done tonight. She shook her head, working to clear the nauseating emotions that flooded her mind and stomach.

She loved her mother, it was true. And Billy, and if she was forced to admit it, Fergus too. But that house, the memories. Nellie. It always took a while to regroup after a call from home. She'd stay the night, Christmas Eve. Why she even pretended she'd drive up to Ellesmere Port and back in one day she didn't know. Her preference to just stay in Exeter was irrelevant in the face of her mother's grief; she'd never recovered after Nellie. No one had.

Rising from her chair Harriet screwed the cap back on the bottle of wine and returned it to the fridge. She pulled some dark chocolate digestives from the cupboard and boiled herself a cup of tea before settling back at her desk to read through the case files she'd dug up that afternoon, after meeting with Eloise.

Time to research the case law, she thought to herself as she opened the first volume and began to work.

6: The parents

A week later Dorothy and Paul Lane sat in Harriet's office on Exeter's North Street. They'd sought her out for their daughter's defence on recommendation from her boss, John Wykle, the lead partner at Wykle and Norton Solicitors.

'We used to go fishing together,' Paul smiled as he shook Harriet's hand firmly. She indicated for them to take a seat and settled down behind her wide oak desk. 'Before he moved up from Salcombe, to take the partnership here,' he finished. Memories of happier summer days flitted over the faces of Dorothy and Paul, a moment of respite that vanished almost as swiftly as it came. 'But when all this trouble with Eloise came up, he was the first person I thought of for help. And he insisted you were the one for the job.'

Harriet nodded. *Trouble* was one way of putting it, not the word Harriet would have chosen. 'John has been like a mentor for me here at Wykle and Norton. I appreciate his vote of confidence,' she said, taking a moment to observe her clients. They sat straight, shoulders tight, mirroring each other's tension and uncertainty. Dorothy was small and neat, dressed in a matching shirt and cardigan outfit, hair grey but styled, her lined face tight against her bones, eyes slightly widened. Paul was broad of shoulder and tall. He looked strong for his age, sorrow limning his pale blue eyes. Eloise's eyes, Harriet realised.

She plunged right in, 'I have reviewed your daughter's case file so far. Though there will be more from the DPP in the coming months as we await the Committal Hearing.' She paused, scanning the faces before her, noting the glimmer of hope within their eyes. *Time to get real*, she thought, before continuing. 'On the evidence gathered so far: your daughter found covered in Mr Huxley's blood; the weapon being her crafting scissors and the letter from the Family Court requesting mediation for Mr Huxley to take custody of Jacob, it doesn't look good for Eloise.'

Dorothy shifted in her seat, hands clamped tightly in her lap. Harriet waited, but the mother said nothing. She continued, 'Coupled with your elder daughter, June's testimony that she was away at precisely the time of the murder and arrived home to find Eloise hysterical… The DPP will argue Eloise is guilty by reason of means, motive and opportunity. On the evidence so far, it is likely the prosecution will succeed. The defence of those allegations will be difficult. There is not, at this time, a basis to argue she is wholly innocent. '

Paul took in a sharp breath, burrows frowning. Tears were forming in Dorothy's eyes, her lips quavering. Harriet gave them a moment, letting the stark reality sink in. She didn't believe in false hope. Just the facts and the truth they revealed. Facts were everything.

'But there may be an opportunity to argue culpability. Eloise has no memory of the event. And June has stated she was in Devon, living at your beach house, as a means of recovery from post-natal depression. If we can build a case to show Eloise was not of sound mind, or was unaware of the actions she took, she does not have the mens rea, or the mental element necessary to be found guilty of the crime. We might be successful in arguing Eloise is not guilty by reason of insanity. Having met with Eloise at The Orchard, I feel this to be the safest course of action. Psychiatric facilities can have a dark reputation, but The Orchard is a calm place. Somewhere Eloise can get the help she needs.'

A wobbly 'oh' sounded from Dorothy as the tears finally won over her composure and she buried her face in her hands. Paul placed a stoic hand on his wife's hunched back, but his eyes did not leave Harriet's face.

'It would mean being detained in a mental hospital for the criminally insane, at the Queen's Pleasure. Not a set sentence. But she would receive treatment and help for her illness,' Harriet explained

'The alternative?' Paul asked, voice low.

'Prison, High Security Prison. Life sentence, parole in 20, maybe. The nature of the crime was… heinous.'

'Eloise can't go to prison!' Dorothy cried, 'My baby can't. She's too fragile, she wouldn't survive!'

'Calm Dorothy,' Paul said, hand still at her back.

Dorothy sobbed again and Paul shuddered. Harriet suppressed a flash of guilt. She'd been blunt, but they had to face the reality of the situation Eloise faced.

Paul fixed Harriet with his pale eyes. 'Eloise has always been unsettled, mentally I mean. Dorothy had some, difficulties, with pregnancy after June. Eloise took a while to come along, it's why the girls are so far apart. When Lou did come, she was early, sickly and small. She grew into an anxious child, prone to fancies. June would tease her, 'you'd find something to worry about in paradise,' she'd say.' He paused, taking a deep breath. 'Eloise was committed into the psychiatric ward at Hollydale when she was 15. For six months. Delusions, she thought her sister was trying to harm her, which was absolutely ridiculous. She was better after that. But we knew she had to stay close, so we could keep an eye on her. '

'Grant seemed to settle her, calm her,' Dorothy took up the tale. 'He was an old friend of June's from their uni days. Seemed a perfect match. But then the troubles with Jacob...'

'Troubles?' Harriet prompted.

Dorothy continued, 'They'd been married five years. Eloise was working as a Medical Secretary in London, Grant was doing wonderfully at Barclays. They seemed, well, happy. But Eloise, she wanted a baby. So did Grant. And despite her youth, she was only 26 when they started trying, they just never fell pregnant. So they invested in IVF. The hormones, the procedures, the embryos that didn't make it,' Dorothy sighed, 'Eloise fell into a deep depression. We suggested she take a break, a year to reset. But she didn't listen...'

'She was right though,' Paul interrupted, 'Jacob came along that year. She just needed the extra time.'

Dorothy's eyes flicked up at her husband, lips pressed tight in irritation. Not a shared opinion then, Harriet surmised. Dorothy continued, 'Lou was so happy. Grant too. Just so happy. And Jacob, he was perfect, a mini Grant. But Eloise... the depression returned, stronger. Grant said he'd come home and find her in bed sobbing, Jacob screaming, his nappy soaked. He hired a nanny to help her, but Eloise just got worse... He said she was impossible.'

'So the weakling ran,' Paul stated, voice flat and dark. 'Left her with her illness and moved in with a friend. A *female* friend.' His tone said just what his opinion on that was. Harriet nodded solemnly.

'She needed help, but after our experience when she was committed... it was a horrid place, we didn't want to put her through that again. So we moved her down to Devon, to be near us.' Dorothy went on, 'We thought the sea air and the quiet would do her some good. And June was wonderful. Cut back her hours at her management business so she could work remotely, and moved in with Eloise to help care for her and Jacob. June has always been a wonderful sister, always protective of Eloise, even now, as adults. She took Eloise for walks, encouraged her to chat with the neighbours. And it seemed to be working. She was doing well.'

'When did Grant start visiting?' Harriet asked.

'Late September, I think,' Dorothy replied. 'Said he wanted to reconcile, that he missed his son...'

'Took him six months to develop a conscience,' Paul said, scathingly.

'He visited on weekends. Eloise lit up. She was like a young girl again, being courted. She seemed so happy. Just the week before she told me she believed they would move back to London together soon...'

'Then the custody letter came,' Paul said.

Harriet consulted her notes, the letter was dated November 8th, one week before the murder.

'Luckily June saw it before Eloise. Rang me when Lou was on one of her walks. We all agreed it was best not to show it to Eloise, not yet. We hoped... well, we hoped Grant could be reasoned with. That we could find another way...'

'Had either of you or June approached Grant in the week leading up to his murder?'

'We hadn't,' Dorothy said, looking to her husband for confirmation. 'And as far as we know neither had June. He only came down for the weekends... so none of us had had the chance.'

'So you are saying that, to the best of your knowledge, Eloise didn't know about the custody application?'

'Oh no, we all agreed not to tell her. She was doing so well. A big shift like that... it would have put her back. The threat to her child, but also the financial burden.'

Paul coughed loudly.

'Financial burden?' Harriet asked.

Dorothy's hands fluttered before her. 'Oh, well, the Huxleys, they pay Eloise an allowance. £400 a fortnight, to support Jacob's care. It comes out of Grant's salary from their Estate. He wasn't too happy about it, but the Huxleys wanted to help support Eloise. The payments allow Eloise to just focus on her health, and Jacob's too of course. But if Grant had sole custody...'

'The payments would stop.'

37

'We were able to help, but only so long. We gave all we could...'

Harriet jotted down some notes, keeping her face neutral. *More motive*, she sighed inside.

The family's subterfuge, however well intended, didn't help Eloise's case either. If she'd found the letter, which was not an unreasonable assumption, how would she have reacted? The police transcript said she flew into a red rage when they showed her the letter... Yet when Harriet had spoken to Eloise she had said she and Grant were working on a reconciliation. As if the letter didn't exist. Curious.

'Did Eloise ever see a psychologist, for her post natal?'

Guilt lit Dorothy's eyes. 'No,' Paul supplied. 'She just needed some rest and time with Jacob. And if that rat had stayed by her side, supported her like a husband should...'

'Peace, dear,' Dorothy whispered softly, placing a hand on her husband's knee. Paul drew in a deep breath and settled. 'A husband is meant to stick around, good times and bad,' he said, 'not cut and run when things get tough. We should have known after what happened with June...'

'June?' Harriet enquired. Paul looked frazzled, eyes shifting side to side.

'It was a long time ago,' he mumbled.

Harriet looked to Dorothy who grimaced. 'June and Grant were together, at University. Not just friends. But things got, complicated. They broke up.'

'And when did Grant and Eloise start seeing each other?'

'Oh, not until mid 2013, nearly a decade later. It was water under the bridge by then.'

Harriet nodded, that was an interesting piece of information, but was it relevant? She filed it away for consideration. Her eyes slid subtly across to check her desk clock. The hour appointment was up. Harriet had a court appearance in two hours and fancied lunch before then. Time to wrap up.

'Mrs Lane, Mr Lane, thank you very much for your time today. It's been most helpful for the case. Eloise is currently being assessed at The Orchard. Once I hear what the psychiatrists have to say about her condition we will have more to go on. Until then, if you think of anything, or have any questions, please don't hesitate to call my office.'

'She's not a murderer, Ms Bell,' Dorothy said suddenly. 'She is a gentle, loving girl. This is not her. She needs help. Not prison, never prison.'

Her eyes locked on to Harriet's, her desperation and hope clear. Harriet nodded. 'When I know more I will be in touch.'

'Thank you,' Paul said, settling his hand on the small of Dorothy's back and leading her to the door.

Harriet leaned back in her chair watching the Lanes depart. They were sincere, she thought. Honest, hard working people who loved their daughters. Did that love blind them from an evil side to Eloise? Or was she really as sweet and gentle as she seemed? Her motives did seem to be piling up: the threat to Jacob, the loss of income. The DDP's assertion that she found the custody application and, threatened by the loss of her child she flew into a rage, was very strong. It explained the trigger for the fugue, for leaving Jacob alone. Alone facing such betrayal her mental instability would reasonably be triggered. Yet, could she be said to have had a motive for murder at all if she couldn't even remember doing it?

Paul's anger towards Grant was interesting. Motive enough for murder? No, that was a long shot. The scissors, the blood on Eloise, there would have been evidence he had been there too. She shook her head. She rather understood Paul's disgust with Grant. Try as she might Harriet couldn't muster any sympathy for the victim. A man who deserted his wife when she was ill, who then wooed her with kind words, only to conspire behind her back to take her child. There was obviously more to the story of his relationship with June. And Paul had all but confirmed Grant had been unfaithful to Eloise. Only the once? Doubtful. There was definitely more background here to investigate. Harriet wouldn't mind betting there was more than one woman out there who was angry at Grant Huxley.

7: Bloody Christmas

Christmas Eve started early, the drive to Ellesmere Port was a long one and Harriet wanted to avoid the holiday traffic. Loading her car with her overnight bag and gifts for her family: whiskey for dad, though God he didn't need it; hand creams for mum and bluetooth ear buds for Billy, Harriet double checked her laptop was secure. Sighing she climbed into her Mazda and began the trek. The dark blue of pre-dawn languidly melted to deep cobalt and then pale cerulean as she veered onto the M5.

As expected the four hour drive took more like six, traffic. As Harriet pulled into her parents' short drive on Thornton Road, her stomach growled a protest at its emptiness, her eyes crusty and strained. Packed tightly against the properties on the rest of the street, the off cream exterior of the terraced house bubbled around the windows. The front lawn, a shining testament to her mother's skills in summer had been reduced to a muddy puddle by the constant rains of the festive season. Anne, dressed in jeans and a thick woollen jumper, Santa Clause grinning from the stitching, dutifully met her on the wet drive, despite the misting damp that drifted down from the grey skies overhead. The air was thick with the desire to drop its watery burden.

'Mum,' Harriet smiled as Anne enfolded her in a tight embrace, warm against the December cold.

'Lunch is ready for the table, we waited for you. I don't want to miss a moment with you, seeing as our time is so short.'

Harriet turned to her car and rolled her eyes, ignoring the first of many not-so-subtle jabs she knew she would have to endure from her mother during this visit. She pulled her bags from the boot and followed her mother into her childhood home. The hallway was dim, masking the worn carpet that covered the frustratingly small steps to the second floor bedroom, steps that once matched her little feet like they were made for her, now outgrown. Just like she'd outgrown the whole house and the town it sat in. Harriet trudged upstairs to her room. Dumping her bags Harriet stretched her shoulders and striped off her t-shirt and jumper. Donning a white shirt and cream cardigan set, she headed for the bathroom, splashed some life back into her face and checked her eyes for sleep before heading for the dining room below.

The room was bedecked with Christmas cheer. A bright red runner trimmed with reindeer divided the dinning table in two, tiny plastic Christmas trees at either end, and a plastic Santa lamp held court from the side table. There was silver tinsel hanging from the ceiling and Christmas bunting, made by Nellie, Billy and Harriet as children, lined the doorway to the kitchen. Harriet suppressed a shudder. Lord but she hated Christmas time.

Her brother's wiry frame sat at the table. He smiled at her as she entered, saluting her with his Carlsberg. Her father, who was sitting in his lounge chair, maintaining the heavy groove of his butt in the worn fabric, TV blaring the latest Premier League standings in preparation for the Boxing day matches, didn't stir. Smoke curled up from the chair. Harriet frowned, still smoking inside. *Bloody hell.*

Her mother came pacing from the kitchen, bringing forth the scent of roast chicken and potatoes and placed her offerings on the red table runner. 'Lunchtime,' she called across the room to her husband. Fergus raised a hand to signal he'd heard, stubbed out his cigarette on his fancy metal ashtray and pressed the raised top. The metal lid swirled, flinging the ash into the bowl of the tray, lid closing above it. A gift from Harriet, thinking putting the ash inside the tray would help with the smell. She hadn't accounted for the smoke infused furniture and closed windows. But her father was at least using it. A small smile played on her lips.

Fergus rose from his chair and muted the TV. Bringing the remote with him he turned, finally acknowledging Harriet's arrival.

'Ah there's my girl,' he beamed, stretching thick workman's arms out wide for a hug as he advanced towards her. Harriet allowed herself to be pulled into his embrace, breathing in his scent of car grease, smoke and stale beer. Nothing changed. Fergus pulled back and eyed his daughter, jaw working like he had something to say.

'Come on,' her mother interrupted, 'it's getting cold.'

Fergus released Harriet with a pat on the shoulder and took up his place at the table next to her brother, facing across the room towards the ever present sport channel. Harriet sat across from her sibling, her mother at the table head between them. No one blocked Fergus' view of the football round ups.

'This looks delicious mum,' Harriet said. 'How will you top it for tomorrow?'

'Your mother always saves the best for Christmas, Harriet. But every meal is a star,' Fergus stated simply.

Anne busied herself scooping potatoes and slices of chicken onto plates, and passing them round. But Harriet could see the pride that flitted over her face.

'Long drive?' her brother asked.

'The traffic is always heavy for the season,' her mother began, 'never good to be on the roads on Christmas Eve. Better to come up a few days before, I always say.'

Her brother grinned mockingly across the table at Harriet. She kept her face neutral and reached for some honeyed carrots.

'Your mother tells me you have a big new case,' her father took up the conversation.

'Yes, a murder in Devon...'

'Not the husband killer? The mental one on the telly?' her brother exclaimed.

Harriet paused, slowly pouring gravy over her plate as she sought for an answer. 'Well, actually yes, that's the one.'

'Aw Hare,' her brother crooned, 'ain't no case there. We've all seen the news. She was going to kill the baby next. That's well worse than the fucking whore job earlier in the year.'

'Language,' Anne tried.

'How can you defend that?'

Harriet bristled. The media in this country had a *lot* to answer for. The stories that had swirled after the tabloids got hold of the details of Eloise's arrest, specifically about Jacob, had been vindictive and salacious. Nothing to do with public interest. And the coverage comparing Eloise to Stacey Stripp was outrageous, how do you get a fair trial with that kind of thing circulating? Just because they were both women in Devon, who stabbed a man to death. Irrelevant, the cases were totally different. But that shit stuck, no matter what a judge instructed the jury.

'It's not just about guilt and innocence. There is also culpability.'

'What?'

Harriet rolled her eyes, it wasn't worth it. 'Everyone deserves a defence,' she answered evasively.

'Everyone with money,' her brother countered darkly, hooded eyes boring into her face. 'Besides, the truth is pretty obvious.'

'I don't need the truth,' Harriet smiled sweetly at Billy, 'I only need doubt.'

'Wine, Harriet?' her mother asked, proffering a bottle of Sainsbury's Pinot Grigio. 'Please,' Harriet nodded.

'So, another year, another family gathering. Not brought a fella up Harrie?' her father enquired. He did so casually, chopping into a potato and dipping it in gravy, eyes down. Harriet was not fooled. *Here we go again.* She pursed her lips. *Because having a lawyer as a daughter isn't enough,* Harriet thought angrily. *She needs to breed to have value.*

'Not this year dad. No time. Work has been busy. Can you pass the Yorkies?' she threw a glance at her brother, pleading. He sat hunched forward, chewing, grim amusement on his face as he passed the plate of puddings.

Her father sat back as though stretching his belly out. 'Still,' he said. Harriet braced herself. 'You aren't getting any younger. Getting to the 'now or never' for kiddies Harrie. Need to get on to that. There's always work. There ain't always time for family.'

Harriet ignored her brother's smirk. She pressed her eyes closed and counted to ten.

'So how are things at the factory?' she asked, eyes boring into her brother. His grin fell.

'Looking more broadly now,' Billy answered. 'Can't work cars my whole life.'

Harriet tried to mask her surprise, catching her mother's warning glance.

'Don't see why not,' her father said as he chewed at a large slice of chicken. 'Kept food on this table and a roof over your head.' He thumped the table with a fist and stabbed his gravy covered fork towards his son.

Billy's turn to squirm. 'Yeah, I know dad. And it's been a great job. But with Crystal pregnant I need something more than the casual hours…'

'Pregnant?' Harriet exclaimed.

Billy's smile turned positively feral. 'Just three months. We'll be moving in together once she gets her council flat in Liverpool. Yep, gonna be a father.'

'We are all so pleased,' her mother beamed. 'Our first grandchild.'

'You'll have to make time for a mid-year visit, Harrie. To meet your new niece or nephew,' her father said.

Harriet felt her fingers shaking, swallowed hard. Why hadn't her mother said?

Regrouping she faced her brother. 'Congratulations, Billy, that's wonderful news. Will Crystal be joining us tomorrow? I'd love to meet her.'

'Nah, spending Christmas with her parents in town. Maybe next year.'

Lunch continued, butter cake was served, wine poured. As the light began to bleed from the sky her father returned to his chair, cigarette in hand, Billy and two beers in tow. Harriet drifted to the kitchen to help her mother wash up.

'You didn't tell me about Billy and Crystal,' Harriet said, 'I didn't realise they were serious.'

Her mother sighed, hands scraping roast chicken crust from the tray, suds to her elbows. 'I didn't think they were. I don't know, but I don't think it was planned.'

Harriet nodded slowly, 'And the factory?'

Her mother flicked her eyes up to Harriet, 'You mustn't tell your father. He thinks it was Billy's choice.'

Harriet stilled, 'I won't say anything.'

Anne rinsed a plate, shoulders tight. 'He was let go. Failed an on site drug test.'

Harriet nearly dropped the glass she was drying. 'Not...'

'No, no, just marijuana.'

Harriet breathed out heavily. 'What was he thinking?' she hissed. 'Working under the influence. He could have hurt someone, hurt himself...'

'Oh rain it in Harriet,' her mother snapped. 'It's not been easy for Billy. You know that. He's never been right since Nellie. We can't all sail through life like you.'

Harriet pressed her lips together in a thin line, holding in the screaming rebuttal boiling inside. *It wasn't easy for me either. After Nellie, you fell apart. I picked up the pieces. I made my own way, dragged myself through uni working night shifts on night-fill. I've never had a penny from you or dad. I made myself.* But there was no point. Billy was Billy and Harriet would always be second to the golden son; the sister who lived.

Carefully, Harriet folded the dishcloth over the oven handle to dry. The washing up wasn't finished, but she was. 'Had an early start,' she said, turning for the door. 'Going to take a nap.'

Her mother shot her a guilt laden look, but nodded her head, letting her go. Harriet climbed the stairs, heavy footed and wished to god she hadn't let her mother convince her to stay a night in this stupid house.

Later that evening after dinner, as her family sat inside watching *Love Actually* for the billionth time, Harriet took a bottle of Sav Blanc, imported from somewhere, and headed outside. Rugged in her winter jacket and layers of jumpers she sat on the creaky garden bench that faced the street. The mud at her feet had hardened, the air crisp with the promise of frost or snow. *Perhaps it will be a white winter after all*, she pondered, filling her glass.

She flicked out her mobile and began scanning her emails. It might be Christmas, but the law didn't take a break. Her fingers flew across the keypad and she lost time working through her correspondence.

Footfall pulled her from her screen. Billy stood beside the chair, cigarette glowing in his mouth. 'Shuffle over Hare,' he said.

Harriet clicked off her screen and returned her mobile to her jacket pocket, moving aside to make room for her brother. Billy sat down right on the edge of the bench, knee instantly jiggling against the cold. He sucked in a lung full of smoke and blew it out in Harriet's face. Grinning at her frown, he offered her a drag. She shook her head in refusal. He turned away.

Harriet waited a moment, then, 'Mum told me, about the factory. There's no possibility of a second chance?'

Billy shook his head, releasing a long stream of smoke.

Harriet pressed, 'But you can still get references right? From your Foreman? You worked there for 10 years without incident, that's got to count for something.'

Billy looked at her, full in the face, dark eyes glittering in the pale moonlight.

'You haven't even asked if I did it,' he said.

Harriet held his stare, daring him to deny the truth. Billy huffed a laugh, 'Innocent until proven guilty hey?' he drawled.

'A drug test is pretty convincing evidence.'

Billy looked away, staring out at the dark, cold night.

He relented. 'I fucked up. There's no way back. But Mike knows a garage guy in Liverpool who's looking for extra hands. Should be in there.'

'Or you could think about other avenues. You finished your A levels.'

'I'm almost 30, Hare and I'm having a baby. I gotta get a job.'

'There's always some reason why you won't do further study... I got it, before. You had to get clean. But that was years ago now Billy. You could...'

'You barely even have your accent anymore.'

Harriet was pulled up short by the change of topic, 'I haven't lived here in almost 15 years Billy. Accents fade.'

'Sure.'

'Billy...'

'You can't fucking help it can you?' Billy interrupted, face swinging back to hers. 'You just think you're better than us.' He gestured towards the front window, TV light playing across the drawn curtains. 'Better than me.'

Fury blazed in Harriet's chest. *Fucking little shit*, she thought. 'I don't think I am better than you Billy,' she said, voice firm and cold. 'I think *you* are better than *you*.'

Billy eyed her in the dark, expression unreadable. The silence stretched. Finally, he shrugged. 'Whatever, 'night dickhead,' he said and walked inside leaving Harriet alone to ponder the Christmas Eve sky.

January

8: Ruined sanctuary

Harriet stood at the top of the cliff between Torcross and Beesands looking down at the small hotel where Grant Huxley had taken his last breath. The sea glowed in the pale January sun, its rays twinkling on the wooly ripples in the bay. Farmland bordered by trees swept down to the beach, the grasses brown, ice glinting from the shadows. Spring would be beautiful here, Harriet realised, imagining the green pastures full of vibrant yellow flowers contrasted against the bright blue skies of May and June. She turned back, the ice wind whipping at her exposed nose and cheeks, turning them pink from cold. The ground beneath her crunched, flecks of ice in the hardened dirt track cracking beneath her weight. Pulling her shoulders in to shrink the surface area of her body exposed to the winds, Harriet headed back towards Torcross, retracing the walk Eloise took that night; after killing her husband.

She'd arrived early, the drive from Exeter shorter due to the lack of traffic the January gloom inspired. Though it was a sunny day, the wind was unforgiving and people, it seemed, were content to stay indoors. Strolling along the Torcross foreshore she noted the holiday houses boarded up against the storms and wild seas that winter brought, hockey ties and padlocks holding shutters firm against the promise of waves splashing up against them. Only the pub on the edge of the pebbled beach remained open. She turned up the road into the seaside holiday town. Curls of smoke floated from the chimneys of several houses, the few who stayed resident year round keeping warm against the harsh season. The scent was welcome and comforting, conjuring memories of the taste of soup and tawny port.

Harriet pulled her coat tighter about her shoulders and quickened her pace. Shadows lengthened around her as she approached Eloise and June's beach hideaway on Hiddley Drive. The house stood back from the road, a wilderness of bushes and trees blocking a clear view into the home. Nestled, secure. She paused a moment looking out across the Slapton Ley Lake and the waves of the beach beyond. *Stunning view from here*, she thought. Harriet checked her watch, almost four, close enough for her appointment with her client's sister. Yet the driveway stood empty. Perhaps June was running late. She'd check anyway. Striding to the front door, clearly freshly painted in a deep forest green, Harriet knocked firmly.

A squeal of delight sounded from inside, followed by the patter of small fast moving feet.

'Jacob, wait!' a woman's voice called. The door swung open. A tall, statuesque woman stood in the hallway, one hand on the door, the other clasping the shoulder of a toddling boy. Dark eyes looked up at Harriet from behind a mess of blonde curls before the boy ducked behind the leg of the woman. Pudgy hands covered in something shiny gripped her jeans. Harriet looked up at the woman.

'You must be Harriet? I'm June.'

June Lane thrust a hand out to Harriet, saw the slick of jam on her index finger, retracted her hand wiping it on her jean clad leg before returning it in welcome. Harriet took it, shaking gingerly. Still sticky.

'Come in,' June said, bending down and sweeping the small boy into her arms and heading inside. 'Shut the door behind you.'

Harriet stepped across the threshold from the cold of early January and into the warmth only the homes of small children radiated. She closed the door firmly behind her and followed the pale little face that bumped up and down as it watched her over June's shoulder. They entered into a large, open-plan living area, kitchen to the right, lounge and dining combined to the left. June deposited the boy on a kid-sized couch in the middle of the lounge, flicking the TV on to a children's program and, plucking a bottle from the couch, placed the blue plastic cup into the child's waiting hands. The boy settled back, bottle tipped to his lips, large eyes glued to the bright colours dancing across the screen.

'Should give us a few minutes of peace,' June said. 'Tea? Coffee?'

'Tea, thank you,' Harriet said following June to the small kitchen, the warmth of a cup would be welcome after her coastal trek. June flicked on the kettle and leaned against the bench, eyes trained on the TV child. Satisfied, she turned to Harriet.

'Thank you for seeing me,' Harriet began.

'Of course,' June said, 'anything to help Lou. Though I am not sure there is much more I can tell you. The police interviews were very thorough.'

Harriet nodded, removing her coat. 'Oh, sorry,' June said, 'I keep it like a furnace in here. Jacob's had a cough, I don't want it to get any worse. Just throw it over a chair and take a seat at the table. I'll be through with the tea soon.'

Harriet walked back into the lounge-dining room and perched at the table, watching the small blonde head sink sleepily into the cushioned chair.

June placed a steaming cup before her. Harriet wrapped her hands around the mug and smiled her thanks. She let June settle before, 'The Prosecution are making noises about seeking a guilty verdict and prison time.' She paused, letting that sink in. June swallowed some tea, her forehead creased, 'But...'

Harriet continued, 'The psychiatric assessment agreed that Eloise was unstable, but that her condition seems, temporary. Episodes that come and go. It's not what I hoped for. Much easier to argue insanity as a constant rather than as something fleeting.' Harriet sipped her tea.

'So how can I help you?' June said. Harriet observed her face. It was Eloise's, though several years older, and much more sleep deprived. Her pale skin looked drawn and tired. Deep, dark smudges hung beneath her blue eyes. June ran a shaking hand through her bleached locks, exposing a small white scar at her hair line. She caught Harriet's glance at the tiny imperfection.

'Childhood accident,' she said, fingering the white mark. 'I was teaching Lou to skim rocks down at the beach here. We always summered in Torcross. She kept practicing while I swam. I caught a stray pebble.'

'Painful.'

'Not really, more trouble than pain. Eloise cried about it for days, she was so wracked with guilt...'

She stopped, a sad smile on her lips, then looked at Harriet. Waiting.

'I wanted to talk about your relationship with Mr Huxley.' Harriet said simply.

June's eyes narrowed. 'He was my brother-in-law,' she said, tone an unvoiced warning.

'You dated back at Exeter University, did you not? Your mother said things were quite serious.'

June snorted, 'It was uni, nothing was serious. Yes, we went out a few times. Played house at each other's apartments. But it all ended in final year. I moved to Edinburgh for work. I didn't see Grant again until he and Eloise were engaged.'

'And what did you think about that? About your sister marrying your former lover?'

June pursed her lips. 'I didn't think anything,' she said, voice strained. 'It was years ago. Like I said, I hadn't seen him in years.'

Harriet nodded, 'What can you tell me about their marriage? Before Jacob. Did Eloise seem happy?'

'Yes, well, yes. She did. She had a hard time having Jacob but things seemed good. Solid between them.'

'Your father seemed to think he left Eloise for another woman. Do you know anything about that?'

June huffed an impatient breath, 'Aren't you supposed to be helping my sister? Not finding more motives for the bloody police!' she snapped.

'Do you know if he was living with another woman in London after he left Eloise?' Harriet repeated.

June frowned, 'I don't know. It's what I heard, through friends. Why? How does this help Eloise?'

'I'm only considering if there could have been someone else with a motive to hurt Mr Huxley. A lover in London, afraid he would be leaving her, returning to his wife…'

'I don't think that's a strong defence,' June said. 'She was covered in his blood. And he wasn't getting back together with Eloise. He'd applied for sole custody.'

'Eloise didn't know that though, did she?'

'I hid the letter. Mum, dad and I agreed we needed to shield her from it. But we didn't know how to. That bastard!' Her eyes blazed, furious. 'He'd been coming here for weeks, sweet talking, playing happy families… and all the while he was just planning to fuck her over again.'

'You sound very angry.'

'Of course I'm bloody angry!' June's voice rose. She caught herself, eyes flicking to Jacob in the other room. He didn't stir. 'Of course I'm angry,' she repeated, voice controlled but shaking. 'He broke Lou. Deserted her when she needed him most. And he was going to take the last thing she had to hold on to. Jacob.'

'Jacob is Mr Huxley's son too,' Harriet reasoned.

'Not that he fucking cared for six months!' June retorted, her words an echo of her fathers. She blew out a heavy breath, composing herself. 'Look, Grant wasn't all bad. But he wasn't great either. He came first. His career, his money, his wants and needs. Lou is gentle and sweet. She didn't stand a chance against his selfishness.'

'So you weren't happy about their marriage?'

'No, if you must know. I wasn't. But it wasn't my life and there was nothing I could do about it.'

'You say Eloise didn't stand a chance, what do you mean?'

June paused, thoughts turned inward. 'Grant was always going to get what he wanted. She wanted to return to Salcombe, it was where we were brought up, where mum and dad were. But Grant's job in London had to come first. She was fragile, she needed family and friends. But he shoved her into a tiny apartment, left her alone while he was out 'making connections' late into the night. Taking her out with him only occasionally to show off his 'pretty little wife'. He was a bastard. A selfish bastard.'

'Did Eloise complain about his behaviour to you? Did she ever intimate any... rough treatment?'

'You mean did he hit her? No, as far as I know he never raised a hand to my sister. He just... ignored her and when it really mattered, abandoned her. Grant always did put himself first.'

More of that thinly veiled resentment, June was not a fan of Mr Huxley. Mentally, Harriet crossed abuse off the list. A shame, it was getting a lot of traction in the courts these days, especially with the #metoo movement.

'So you can't think of anyone else who would have wanted to harm Mr Huxley?'

June gave a harsh laugh, eyes fixed on the back of Jacob's head, now slumped to the side in slumber. 'Aside from my dad, me and any other woman he'd jilted? No.'

'Be careful saying that Ms Lane.'

'Why? It wasn't me. I was on a bus back from Salcombe when he was killed. 'There but for the grace of God go I,'' she quoted bitterly.

Harriet raised her eyebrows at her.

'I'll be frank,' June said, leaning forward, 'when I saw that custody letter, I saw red. I wanted him gone, out of Lou's life forever. I'm not sorry he's dead. I'm just sorry it was my Lou who did it. She's so gentle and soft. I still can't believe it...' She shook her head and sighed.

'Ms Bell, Lou doesn't remember what happened that night. That's not a lie. When I found her... when I got home she was holding Jacob in her arms, swinging him and singing him to sleep as though it were just any other weeknight. But she was covered in blood. Her hair wet from the rain outside. I thought she was hurt. I never thought...' June closed her eyes, lost a moment in the horror of the memory. 'I ran to her, took Jacob, checked them over. No wounds. I led her to the bathroom to clean her up and I saw the custody letter on the table. That's when I knew...'

'She'd found the letter?' Harriet's eyebrows shot up in surprise. That wasn't what the DPP interviews recorded. They indicated Eloise was surprised by the information. What June was saying worked strongly against Harriet's case. Clear motivation, even if Eloise was now unable to remember it.

'Yes,' June continued, 'I'd left it in the side table drawer. She must've opened it looking for her crafting scissors...'

'The murder weapon? Why would she have been looking for her scissors?'

June looked up startled, 'Well, um, to craft. She always crafts when I'm out.' Her hand tapped on the table top. *She's nervous*, Harriet realised.

'You said you caught the 5:15 p.m. bus from Salcombe, so you would have been home around 6:30 p.m. You came straight home?'

'It was pouring with rain. So yes, straight home.'

'The bus comes in where?'

'By the pub at the beach.'

'Eloise wasn't expecting you for dinner. She said you always visit your parents on Thursdays.'

June shrugged, recovered. 'I do usually see mum and dad on Thursdays. But the car needed a service and I didn't want to leave Lou overnight. So I bussed home. She just forgot I was coming back. She can be forgetful...'

Harriet suppressed an ironic roll of her eyes. Eloise could be forgetful. Understatement.

A little whimper came from the lounge. June stood up and crossed the room to Jacob. Bending she drew a sleepy puddle of child into her arms, cradling him to her chest. Messy blonde curls rested on the curve of her shoulder, face flushed from sleep. One pudgy hand wrapped around the buttons of June's shirt. June pressed her cheek against the small head, rocking Jacob gently as he snuggled. Love radiated from her eyes as she planted a tender kiss on his mussy crown. Harriet shifted awkwardly, the display of open affection so foreign to her own upbringing. A scene of perfect domestic bliss.

'It's Jacob's supper time,' June said. 'If there's nothing more, I will see you out.'

'Just one more thing, if I may. Your mother mentioned the payments that the Huxleys were making, in support of Jacob. Have they continued, given everything that's happened?'

'Yes, Jacob is still their grandchild. The Huxleys are heartbroken, but they love Jacob.'

'I'm sure they do. But how do you access them, with Eloise at St Bernards?'

'The payments come to me. They always have. I manage things here, they understand the situation with Eloise's health.'

'Of course,' Harriet said smoothly.

'Now if that's it?'

Harriet's welcome was well and truly worn out. Standing and collecting her jacket, she smiled, 'I'll ring if I have any further questions.'

Harriet strolled down the street towards the carpark by the pub. The curtains of a nearby house flickered. Nosey neighbours. It was an odd time to be out walking, though, she supposed. Coming to her car she spotted the bus stop by the beachside. Not a long walk, she mused. The pub lights cast a warm glow into the night. It was dark and cold and Harriet was hungry. *Why not?* she decided and headed for the bar. The entrance faced the sea, waves pushing gently against the icy coast. She stepped down into the pub, low ceilinged, dark wood, warm lighting; the smell of fish and pie had her mouth watering and her tummy grumbling in an instant. A few tables were taken up by older, merry-looking men and women. A middle aged man with dark hair waved a welcome, 'Take a seat anywhere love. I'll be with you shortly.'

'Thank you,' Harriet called, removing her jacket and making her way into the heart of the cozy establishment. She chose a seat by the open fireplace and pulled out her mobile phone. As her fingers danced across the keypad, a young girl arrived at her elbow, 'Meal and tonight's specials. Can I get you a drink to start?' she said.

'Just a soda water please,' Harriet answered. She still had a long drive home.

The girl shuffled off and Harriet perused the menu. *Can't pass up fish and chips by the sea, even in winter,* she thought as she closed the menu. Decision made.

Her soda arrived. Her order taken, Harriet leaned back in her chair flicking through emails, subconsciously processing her interview with June. Her client's sister had seemed tense, uneasy. Eyes darting all about the place. *Then again*, Harriet thought, *she is looking after a child*. She shook her head thinking of the small boy, small children in general really. Jacob really was very cute, his fat hands and little smile. She'd felt her heart tug at the sight of his innocent joy. But did she want that responsibility in her life?

'Here you go love,' a jovial voice cut into her reverie as a steaming pile of battered fish fillets and a mountain of hot chips were placed before her.

'Wow!' she said, 'Thank you. What a feast.'

'Can't have our guests going hungry,' the man grinned down at her, his eyes warm.

Harriet smiled. He didn't move away. Harriet looked up, open faced.

'Sorry,' he began, 'but are you the lawyer defending Eloise?'

Harriet startled, 'Yes, but how…'

'Don't get many out-of-towners this time of year,' he shrugged. 'Mighty sad story,' he continued, 'and unlucky too. The only night her sister wasn't there…'

'June was never home on Thursdays. She visited her parents in Salcombe.'

'That what she told you, hey?' He gave a rueful laugh. 'Then why does my daughter see her down at Beesands every Thursday afternoon?'

Harriet looked up in honest surprise. 'I'm sorry,' she said, 'I didn't catch your name?'

'Chris Simons. My daughter, Mason, works at the Beesands hotel. She found the body.'

Harriet blinked, small world. 'And you are saying your daughter has seen June at the Beesands hotel?'

'Every week on Thursdays, since that wayward husband started coming down for the weekends.'

'I thought Grant only arrived on Friday night?'

'No, Thursday was check in, just before June arrived. Mason often took them room service, sometimes he ate alone in the dining room when June left.'

'But why…'

Chris gave her a wicked wink, 'I think we all know the answer to that one don't we? Shame though, the one night she's not there… unlucky for the guy. I mean, Grant was a total bastard, but no one wishes that on him. Anyway, your fish is getting cold, I should leave you in peace. Can I get you some vinegar, sauces?'

Flustered, Harriet stumbled, 'Um, yes, vinegar please.'

Chris strolled away to get the condiments. Harriet stared at her heaped plate of fish, thoughts spinning. June was having an affair with Grant? Could it be true? Harriet knew they had been a couple back in their university days, but the family seemed sure that was in the past. And just this afternoon she'd expressed such strong disgust at Grant's treatment of Eloise, which really didn't fit with this revelation. Was it just the gossip of a small town, or was there something to it? June had seemed nervous… Was it the affair she wanted to hide, or something more?

Either way, June's place as the 'reliable witness' would be somewhat undermined if the rumours were true.

Chris returned with a basket of sauces, 'Here you go,' he smiled. He turned to leave, then paused, 'Don't suppose you ever worked out who the little white car belonged to?'

'Little white car?'

'Yeah, Mason said it was parked in June's spot. From her description, not one I've seen around before, so not a local. Police asked Mason if a guest had checked in with it, but it didn't belong to someone staying at the hotel.'

'I've not heard, sorry,' Harriet's mind was racing. The Prosecution hadn't mentioned an unaccounted for vehicle…

'Ah well, you enjoy your fish now,' Chris smiled and lumbered off.

On automatic Harriet picked up her knife and fork, but her appetite had evaporated. This case just wasn't sitting right. Yes, the evidence seemed clear, Eloise's finger prints and DNA, her mental state, June's testimony, but… *but what?* Harriet prompted herself.

But something just didn't *fit*.

Eloise thought she and Grant were reconciling, she didn't know he would be in Beesands that night. Did June? Were they really having an affair? Everyone said Eloise was gentle and kind. And… and, when Harriet looked into her eyes, she saw honesty and truth, not a killer. June, on the other hand, seemed edgy, strained. And now an unaccounted for car. It was probably nothing, but it showed the DPP weren't being above board, they'd left out some details. What else had they omitted?

She might not have all the answers yet, but she sure had something.

Ammo, Harriet grinned. *There is more to this case,* she thought. *And I'm going to find out what.*

9: To play the game

Harriet's heels clacked loudly, echoing down the hallway of Lees Chambers Exeter. She'd woken early this morning, taken care in preparing her appearance: black tailored suit, modest length skirt, tiny pearl earrings. Minimal makeup, hair pulled back in a slick ponytail. Heels: high. She strode briskly, heels striking the tiled floor confidently, face impassive. Harriet was meeting with the DPP on the Lane-Huxley case, Stephanie Emmetts. She had never appeared opposite Stephanie before, but her reputation as a viper proceeded her. 25 years in the job hardened a person. This meeting would be an hour of posturing and intimidation.

Harriet paused at Stephanie's office door and squared her shoulders. Taking a deep breath she knocked. Without waiting for an invite she stepped through the door, stomach flipping.

She loved this part.

Stephanie looked up sharply from her desk, whipping off her glasses and leaning forward in her chair.

'Well, come in then,' she said, voice cool as she gestured to the chairs before her desk. Harriet stepped confidently to the desk and took a seat. Stephanie's eyes, lined by experience, surveyed her across the heavy wooden desk from beneath a brow peppered with grey. She steepled her hands, resting her head on her finger tips, her sharp brown gaze measuring Harriet in silence as she shuffled her shoulders adjusting the fall of her silky cream shirt. Harriet sat straight and returned her stare, unfazed. The corner of Stephanie's mouth quirked up and the older woman leaned into her chair back, hands now resting on the table top.

'Ms Bell.'

'Ms Emmetts.'

'Thank you for coming,' Stephanie began, voice efficient. 'It seemed a good time to discuss the direction of this case, given the report from The Orchard…'

'Eloise Lane-Huxley has been an exemplary inmate,' Harriet said. 'Doctor Taylor says she is responding well to treatment.'

'A little too well, wouldn't you say?' Stephanie raised a thick eyebrow and flashed Harriet the briefest of smiles. 'Her memory of the days leading up to, and events surrounding, her husband's murder are exceptionally clear. Odd that it is just the event itself she seems to stumble over.'

Harriet remained calm. She would not be rattled that easily.

'She is not of sound mind. The memory lapse makes that clear.'

'Or she simply doesn't want to remember.'

'Finding out your husband has been murdered would be a shock to anyone.'

'"Finding out?" Come now Ms Bell, she had the murder weapon in her hand. She was covered in her husband's blood.'

'The murder weapon fell to the floor, and June Lane was also covered in blood.'

'Ms Lane was indeed covered in the blood of Mr Huxley. From finding her sister in distress. She has a solid alibi. Was on the bus back from Salcombe at the time of the murder. Checked her car into the garage at 4:30 p.m. We confirmed of course.'

'Doesn't prove it was Eloise who killed Mr Huxley.'

A slow smile spread across Stephanie's brown face. She leaned forward, eyes glinting. 'Her finger prints were found on the scissors. Her DNA in Grant Huxley's room.'

'So was June's,' Harriet said, probing. Had the DPP heard the rumours about June and Grant?

Stephanie waved a hand in dismissal, 'Easily explained. The sisters live together, their jackets on the same rack sharing hair follicles, the scissors could reasonably have been be used by both sisters. And again, June Lane was in Salcombe that afternoon…'

'So you checked she caught the bus? Found a witness?'

Stephanie blinked. Before she could open her mouth to reply, Harriet continued, 'She didn't, say, hire a car from the garage for the evening, to return home? It was a very timely bus route…'

'A bus left Salcombe station at 5:15 p.m., Ms Bell…'

'So who was driving the white car then?'

Stephanie's eyes narrowed.

Got ya! Harriet thought.

Harriet paused, settling back into her seat comfortably. Stephanie stared at Harriet in silence. Harriet could feel her tension, her years of experience trained on Harriet with laser focus, aiming to intimidate. Harriet kept her face neutral, eyes level with Stephanie's. Waiting. She would make Stephanie ask...

'What...'

'There was a small white car in the carpark of the Beesands Hotel, seen at around 5:30-5:45 p.m. on the night Mr Huxley was murdered. I double checked with the hotel staff, it wasn't registered to a guest.' Harriet paused, letting her meaning sink in. 'So who else was in the area on the night Mr Huxley was murdered?'

Stephanie leaned forward in a practiced languid motion, lips twisting into a nasty grin. 'You're reaching, Ms Bell.'

Well no shit, Harriet thought, but she kept her face calm. 'All *I* need to do is plant doubt, Ms Emmetts. It seems a simple check for you to do to rule out another possible culprit. Who else was in the area? Who owns a white car? Strange you have overlooked it.'

'We have DNA...'

'And I have a client who is not of sound mind. She has no recollection of the events of the night of November 15th, has no recollection of walking to Beesands, or killing her husband. In fact, she thought they were getting back together. She does not have the requisite mens rea and is Not Guilty by Reason of Insanity. '

'That's arguable.'

'So argue it,' Harriet stood up, walking for the door. She paused turning back to Stephanie Emmetts, 'But I advise you make sure of *all* your facts before you decide to take that route.'

Stephanie settled back, smirking darkly at Harriet. 'I've many more years in this game than you, little one,' she said. 'It takes more than misdirection to plant the seed of doubt into the mind of a jury, or to rattle me.'

'And I've been playing the 'game' long enough to know not to give away all the tricks up my sleeve at once. Good chat Ms Emmetts. See you in court.'

With that Harriet swung the door open and walked out into the hall.

DS Robert Fields sat at his desk in Exeter Police Station going over paperwork, the coffee at his elbow long gone cold. A commotion sounded from the door to the open area office. Loud voices were followed by the entrance of the imposing figure of Ms Stephanie Emmetts striding through the door. She paused momentarily, eyes scanning the desks. Robert grimaced and raised his hand. She was working his case after all. Her eyes caught his movement and narrowed like a hawk hunting prey. Presently, she stood in front of his desk. A tall woman anyway, from his seated position she was positively threatening. 'Ms Emmetts,' he tried.

'We are a team, DS Fields,' she paused.

'Well, yes…'

'That was not a question, DS Fields. It was a statement of fact. One I am sure you would agree with?'

Unsure whether this was now a question, Robert took the safer route and nodded silently.

'And team members work together, do they not? Share information?'

'Yes, of course.'

'All information?' Her eyes blazed.

What was this? Robert thought.

'What's this abou-?'

'Who the fuck does the little white car belong too? And why did I hear about it from fucking Harriet Bell and not you?'

Oh. Robert blanched. *Fuck.*

10: Thursday night

Slumping down on his worn sofa, the now off-duty DS Robert Fields cracked open a beer. Flicking on the TV he took a swig, settling back into the lounge and rubbing his neck. What a rubbish day. He hated working at the Exeter station. Knightsbridge was so much quieter - further for the angry lawyers to travel to berate him. Stephanie Emmetts' furious eyes flashed in his memory. Hell, she made him feel like a school boy again.

'Glad she's on our team,' he said to the empty house around him. 'Cheers to prosecutors.' And swigged another gulp of his lager.

To be fair, she was right. He had been slack with the paperwork on the Huxley case. Well, no, not slack, the car detail just didn't seem important. They had the DNA and the murder weapon, the culprit in prison, or as good as... he shook his head at himself ruefully. After 20 years on the force, he knew that wasn't an excuse. Especially in a murder trial. Every detail mattered. Every. God. Damn. Detail. He just hadn't been himself since Gemma...

The front door squeaked open and slammed shut.

'Oy Oy,' he called out in welcome as his son shuffled into the room, bouncing his football on the floor. 'How was training?'

'Good,' Thomas gifted him the standard monosyllabic answer that teenagers loved and slung his training bag onto the floor.

'Uh, no, laundry,' Robert chided and watched as his son rolled his hazel eyes (Gemma's eyes) and loped across the room to the laundry. At least he still did what he was told... for now.

'Was thinking we might order in tonight.' Robert called across the room to Thomas, 'what do you fancy? Pizza or Indian?'

'I'm good,' Thomas said, emerging from the laundry, ball still in hand. 'Gonna clean up and head round to James'. We've got a project to finish. His mum'll feed me, she said.'

'You asked her that?'

'Nah, she offered. After training when we were chatting.'

'Okay,' Robert nodded, ignoring the pang of guilt that struck his chest. He hadn't been to training in weeks... 'Need a lift?'

'Nah, gonna bike it.'

'It's bloody cold out there Tom,' Robert started.

'All good dad. Got my jacket.' He turned and raced away up the stairs. Soon Robert heard the shhh of the shower. *Bet he leaves his kit on the bathroom floor again*, he thought. But a small smile touched his lips. Thomas was growing up. *I really need to make it to a game, soon*, he resolved. A part of him acknowledged the hollow sensation that opened again in his stomach, the knowledge that it was a false promise he was making to himself. Being a parent just didn't fit in well with his chosen career. Forcing the emotions aside, Robert downed the last of his beer, rose and headed to the fridge for another.

An hour later Robert scraped the last of his microwave lasagne from its plastic packaging, highly underwhelming, and chucked the tray down on the coffee table. The TV blared away before him, some nonsense celebrity challenge show, they looked like they were trying to swim (?) through a puzzle. Robert didn't know and frankly didn't care. He got up and headed to the fridge. No beer left. He paused. *Probably for the best*, he thought and wandered back to the couch, picking up the remote as he slumped back down and flicking through the channels: sport, news, some show with dancing and singing. Shit, when did TV get so bad? He checked the time on his phone: 8 p.m. Thomas would be out for hours yet, he never made it back from James' before midnight. *Probably should do something about that*, Robert thought, without conviction. Two nights out of three when he was on late shift in Knightsbridge, he wasn't here to check anyway... another hazard of being a cop. He scrolled his phone, looking for distraction but could not settle. The huddling of winter was getting to him, he needed to get out, socialise. But it was so cold outside...

Fuck it, he decided. Suddenly energised, he got up and grabbed his jacket, thumbing through his contacts list. He clicked a number, 'Hi there. Yeah it's Rob. Keen for a beer?'

Harriet leaned close to her companion's ear. 'I mean, can you believe it? She was fucking her sister's husband!' Harriet pulled back and took a sip of her wine. The bar music blared over the speakers, making conversation tricky. The beat pulsed through her limbs, the wine sliding down her throat. Damn it felt good to be out.

Phoebe looked at Harriet in mock horror. 'Slut,' she crooned. Harriet laughed.

'It's a fucked up case, Fi,' she shouted to her friend. 'Wanna know the worst bit?'

Phoebe gestured for Harriet to continue. 'I think I like her.'

'Like who? The slutty sister?'

'What? No! Eloise. My client. The murderer. She just seems so.... sweet. I think we would have got along in another life.' *Something just doesn't fit,* she thought to herself. The doubt that had seeded that first day she met Eloise had been growing the more she read about the case…

'That's bull Harrie,' Phoebe laughed, 'you don't mesh well with *sweet.* You're too blunt.'

'I can be gentle.'

Phoebe snorted and held up her empty glass. 'Another round?'

Harriet nodded and watched as Phoebe made her way to the crowded bar, heads turning in unison to ogle her long, slim legs. Harriet turned away, taking in the Thursday clientele with a sweep of her eyes. Smiling faces, black wrapped limbs, heels and fake nails. The Red Lion was a fun bar, always pumping. When Phoebe had suggested after work drinks and then dinner Harriet, still on a high from the success of her meeting with Stephanie Emmetts, had been more than keen. Three hours later and food had yet to be mentioned. Most likely they would grab some fish and chips as they stumbled home from the last bus.

Phoebe was right, it felt good to be out. Work had been all encompassing lately, well fuck, always. Harriet was ready to let off some steam. She watched Phoebe deftly avoid the groping hands of some drunk punter and rolled her eyes. *Fucking men.* She was about to make her way over to play guardian when the pub door opened. A tall man with dark hair and eyes walked in. The corner of her mouth hitched up in a grin. *This should be fun.*

Robert scanned the bar looking for Bobbie. Rob and Bob the 'opposite brothers' so nicknamed by their parents during the boys' primary school years; back in the 80's, when that wasn't a racist thing to say about a white boy and black boy who were friends… maybe? The two were due a catch up, and Robert certainly wasn't in the mood for more police talk after today… He spotted Bobbie in the far corner, chatting to a couple of over made-up blondes. *Typical,* he thought to himself. *Leave the guy alone for a moment and…*

'Hey there Superintendent.'

Robert looked down, surprised to be recognised on this side of town. There before him stood a familiar brunette. 'Ms Bell,' he said, unable to keep his eyes from scanning the petite solicitor in her out of hours leather pants and low cut singlet top. His gaze returned to her face, her eyes shined with recognition and mischief. He knew the little lawyer well, often seeing her at the Magistrates Court in town, sometimes on the opposite side of a committal hearing or mediation. She was new to running her own cases, but rapidly earning a reputation for tenacity. And today, she had brought the wrath of Stephanie Emmetts down upon his head.

'Surprised to see you out,' she smiled sweetly, 'I'd have thought Stephanie would have you locked in the office.'

So she knew it too… Roger returned her smile. 'I can't discuss case matters with you. And you know it,' he said and turned to go.

'You know your star witness is a liar right?' she said to his back. That turned him around.

She grinned wickedly, 'June Lane, the good sister. Taking care of her younger sibling and her nephew… Fucking her sister's husband.'

Roger felt a moment of shock. He hadn't suspected. Keeping his face impassive, he answered lightly, 'Sounds like another motive for us, rather than a defence for you.'

Harriet shrugged, 'Whatever, she's a liar. I can tell.'

A smile tugged at the corner of his mouth, 'Can you now?' He observed the little woman before him, all curves and soft skin, on the outside. All spice and fire within. 'Perhaps you are in the wrong profession then?'

She scowled at that and fixed him with her eyes. 'Everyone deserves a defence,' she retorted.

'What about the truth?'

'I don't need truth,' Harriet countered, 'I only need doubt.' She gifted him a sarcastic smile. 'Anyway, my drink is returning from the bar. Have a nice night, Detective Superintendent.' She pretended to tip a hat to him and spun on a heel, sauntering away.

Robert watched her make her way across the room, watched her quip something to her friend earning her a boisterous laugh, watched her answering wicked grin. He only turned when she glanced back his way, wine glass clutched in her hand and raised a toast to him across the room. He rubbed his neck, suddenly flustered and made his way to Bobbie and the make-up covered blondes.

11: London Square Chambers

The office was large and grey, like an oversized picture frame around the small and wizened figure of Randell Dawes QC. Short, hunched, grey-haired, wrinkled. Yet in his eyes danced a brilliance no one could miss. Sharp, analytical, accurate and, welcoming.

Harriet's nerves had been building in her gut since she received his agreement to take on Eloise's case. It was one of the more challenging tasks of being a solicitor - soliciting. Not in the street walking sense, in the defence sense. She needed a barrister to present in court, to make the case for Eloise. On what Harriet could only describe as a whim, she had contacted the Clerk of London Square Chambers and to her surprise, delight and now significant apprehension, Randell Dawes Queens Counsel was available to take on the Lane-Huxley brief.

'Good is the enemy of great,' Harriet had whispered to herself after setting the date for their first meeting. Who said that? She couldn't remember. But the quote was accurate. If she wanted to be the best, she had to play with the big boys. And where the big boys of defence law were concerned, no one came bigger than Randell Dawes.

So it was no small surprise to Harriet to be welcomed by a warm, almost grandfatherly smile and the offer of tea, as she arrived at London Square Chambers. So used to the posturing and arrogance of barristers only just her senior, she was taken aback by the easy confidence and camaraderie Dawes offered instantly. Now, sitting in a large upholstered chair in his office, Harriet remained alert and ready, but felt more at her ease as well .

Dawes sipped his tea and smiled at Harriet, 'It is most good to meet you in person, Harriet. I must say, your preparation notes so far have covered all bases well. I think we have a strong case here. Wouldn't you agree?'

Harriet, tea cup resting in her lap, replied, 'Yes, I really do. The law seems clear to me and to be on our side. Eloise was not of sound mind when the murder took place. She can't be held responsible.'

Dawes nodded thoughtfully. 'You say the DPP was making noises about rejecting a plea of Not Guilty by Reason of Insanity? Despite their own submission for her to be held at St Bernards?'

'Gaming, I think,' Harriet said. 'Stephanie Emmetts is a somewhat bold opponent. I have not appeared opposite her before. But she has a reputation. She is good. But rough.'

'So I understand. What does the lead psychologist say?' Randell asked.

'Doctor Taylor's report states that Eloise has no memory of the events of the night of November 15. That her temporary amnesia is genuine. But outside of those few hours, her mind is sharp. She does display symptoms of trauma and repeated small periods of time loss, where she loses track of her surroundings.'

'Interesting.'

'I've seen it myself, sir. When I first visited St Bernards she offered to make me tea then remembered she was not in her kitchen.'

Harriet paused, watching Dawes' face as he absorbed this information. He flicked through some notes, casually, without haste and drained his cup. Folding his hands elegantly before him, he cocked his head in thought. Harriet waited. It was as though she could see the cogs turning behind his eyes. Click-click-click.

'I think,' he began, then paused as if assessing his words, 'I think you are correct.'

Harriet's eyebrows shot up. 'Correct, sir?'

'From your notes, though you haven't said it outright, I deduce you are leaning towards a plea of Not Guilty by Reason of Insanity, applying the Automatism defence. The inconsistency of her mental state makes true insanity a difficult line to hold. But the temporary disease of the mind, to be not in control of your actions for a period of time, due to mental illness, that fits well. It is a stronger argument for our position and harder for the DPP to contest. They would have to show her actions were voluntary. We must show she was not in control of her actions. Her amnesia helps this defence. She didn't know what she was doing.'

Harriet's stomach bubbled with pride. She kept her features calm and professional, suppressing the giddy grin that threatened to break out across her face at the praise. She swallowed and replied calmly,

'Yes, I think it's the right defence.'

'Let's focus our efforts there then.' He paused while Harriet pulled out her note book and pen, then continued, 'We need recent precedent and outcomes.'

'I found a precedent for a man found not guilty using automatism. He strangled his wife whilst effectively sleep walking. Eloise wasn't sleep walking, but she was definitely in a dissociative fugue state. And her prior committal to Hollydale shows a history of delusions.'

'Review the witness statements. And develop the timeline for November 15th and her loss of control over her actions.'

Harriet jotted down his directions, then paused. She sat back in her chair. *Should I say it?* She wondered. The words, the doubt bubbled just beneath the surface of her resolve.

Dawes cocked his head and regarded her. 'There is something else? Something you wish to add?'

Harriet's mouth worked, searching for the right words. Doubt defeated her. She shook her head, 'No, no it's nothing.'

Dawes fixed her with a steady gaze, eyes narrowed, 'There is something. I can see it on your face. You'd play poker well, but not this round... Whatever it is, say it. We need to have everything on the table between us, so to speak. It is the only way a real defence team can work.'

Harriet knew that. She may not have worked on a murder before, but all cases needed transparency and the cohesion of the legal team. Still... she took a deep breath, 'It's just that, well, shouldn't we at least consider the possibility that she is innocent? That she in fact *didn't* do it at all.'

There, she'd said it out loud. She stopped, scanning Dawes' face. He gave her nothing. The real poker player had arrived.

'Go on,' he said.

Harriet took a deep breath. 'Meeting with Eloise, she's just so, gentle and calm. I have met violent, angry people, Eloise isn't one of them.'

'"Violent" people being the rapists most young defence lawyers are forced to defend?'

Harriet frowned.

Dawes leaned back, eyes gazing out the large office window that overlooked Chancery Lane. Grey clouds gathered together in the sky, threatening rain. At length he turned back to Harriet, eyes bright. 'Do you know why I took on this case?'

'No,' Harriet shook her head, 'I didn't want to ask and make you change your mind.' She smiled self-consciously, 'Though I did wonder.'

Dawes lips curved in a small, private smile. 'My wife, Ruth, is sick. Early onset dementia. At first I thought I would retire, look after her, but... She's not really present most of the time, if you understand my meaning. Work is my sanctuary, where things are logical. In the mind, not the heart.' He eyed Harriet.

'I'm sorry,' she said softly. This was unchartered ground. A sharing of private history. Harriet didn't have a road map for this. She decided silence was the best way forward, rather than speaking and risking saying the wrong thing.

Dawes continued, 'Thank you, but sympathy is not what I am looking for. I'm giving you context. My wife is the most kind and giving person I have ever known. Her illness however, is not. Fear, confusion, pain, they can change a person. Any person. None of us truly knows who we are under those pressures. Eloise Lane-Huxley is no exception.'

Harriet felt her uncertainty flutter. But was still unconvinced. 'I agree with your overall point. But there are still elements that don't add up. The lack of motive, for instance. Eloise says she didn't know about the custody application, whatever June may now claim. And the physical size difference. Eloise is such a small woman. Grant Huxley was a big man. It's hard to see how she could have overpowered him so effectively, even with the scissors...'

'I mean no disrespect, Harriet, but this is your first murder case. Against the standard client: aggressive, hormone-fuelled men, who commit acts of violence and violation, someone like Eloise Lane-Huxley is hard to accept as a criminal. But looks can be deceiving. It's easy to fall under your client's spell. Especially when they are a young, pretty woman,' he paused, smiled gently. 'We have to work the facts, not our emotions. And the facts point to Eloise and Automatism. So we work the case.'

Harriet took a deep breath, 'Yes, but...'

Dawes held up a hand, 'I am not against keeping an open mind, Harriet. In defence that would be the fast track to failure. Keep your ear to the ground. Double check the evidence. But work the facts. Only the facts. Are we in agreement?'

'Yes,' Harriet conceded. It was a direction, but with room to move. He hadn't fully shut her down, just reminded her to stay on track. Harriet could work with that. 'Work the facts,' she agreed.

'Good. Well, I think that is enough for today. I'll expect an update from you in the next two weeks.'

'I'll email through the documents as I have them prepared.'

'Excellent. Good day Ms Bell.'

Harriet stood and they shook hands, before she headed for the door.

'Oh and Harriet?' she paused and turned, 'Facts are king, it's true. But instinct has a place. Use it, but don't rely on it.'

Harriet smiled, nodded and left.

She took her time returning to Paddington, choosing to stroll down Chancery Lane towards the Thames before heading to her station. Her route took her past one of the famous Inns of Court of inner London, the professional association for barristers across England and Wales. Lincoln Inn sprawled down one side of the street, red brick walls and heavy black gates tall and authoritative. The sight itself felt like knowledge. Harriet remembered the first time she saw the Inns - the sense of grandeur and wonder, the feeling of being in the presence of an unattainable level knowledge and skill. How she longed to walk those grounds, not as a tourist, but as a peer.

Now, almost ten years later, as she made her way to Embankment Station, the words of Randell Dawes QC still cycling through her mind, for the first time, she felt she just might be worthy of such an establishment. Determination lengthened her stride. Harriet wanted a place at the Bar, a membership to an Inn, an office in a Chambers in London. She wanted it all, and somehow, she was going to get it.

She turned along the river, grey and wild in the January winds. This great place of commerce and discovery churned before her eyes, yet she did not see. In her mind sat only one goal: to find the truth of what happened to Grant Huxley. To build a rock solid case to defend Eloise Lane-Huxley. And to prove herself ready for London.

February

12: Delayed Trauma

Eloise looked pale today. Her blue eyes wide, pupils dilated.

'How are they treating you?' Harriet asked.

Eloise curved her lips in a gentle smile. 'Everyone is so nice here, the nurses especially. Nothing like Hollydale,' she paused, a shadow drifting across her features. Then, shaking her head as if to clear her thoughts, continued, 'Doctor Taylor is very encouraging. He says I'm making wonderful progress. It's nice, to have help.'

Her blue eyes flickered, face suddenly unsure. 'Not that I didn't have help before, of course,' she said quickly. 'My sister, June, she was just amazing after Grant left. She's so good with Jacob. It was his birthday last week…'

She trailed off.

It was the third time Harriet had met with her client. Eloise remained gentle and kind, and prone to concerns that she had said the wrong thing, offended someone or something. Always polite, asking after Harriet, she genuinely seemed to care that Harriet was well and happy. It made a nice change from the leers of rapists and misogyny of domestic abusers. Who'd have thought a murderer would be her preferred client?

'Can we talk about that time, Eloise? When you were in Hollydale.'

Eloise shifted uncomfortably in her metal framed chair, bit her lip. 'What do you want to know?'

Harriet paused, reviewed her notes. *Start small*, she decided. 'You were 14 when you were committed, correct?'

A nod.

'You were resident for… 10 months? Do you remember what treatment you received?'

Eloise pressed her eyes closed, her head gave a short shake, more like an involuntary tick then a chosen action. 'Um… counselling and, some other therapies.'

Harriet watched her client, her distress clearly filling up the room. Time for a new tack. She smiled gently, 'You obviously did very well, Eloise. 10 months wasn't a long stay.'

That was a guess, in truth Harriet had no idea how long the average treatment time was in mental hospitals.

Eloise smiled back, eyes thankful, 'I always try my best,' she said.

'Yes, you do.' Harriet closed her folder, leaning forward. 'Eloise, your father mentioned to me that one of the reasons you were committed was because you feared that your sister was going to hurt you. Can you tell me about that?'

She recoiled, hands pulling into her lap, shoulders hunched forward, instinctually protecting her vulnerable core. 'I had delusions.'

'What did you see, in these delusions?'

'They were just made up visions. Like bad dreams. They weren't real.'

'Bad dreams that June did what?'

'Just… hit me and things like that.' Eloise waved her hand in a vague gesture. 'I understand they weren't real, now.'

Harriet cocked her head, taking in her client, 'Do you remember what triggered these, visions?'

As though trying to produce saliva in a dry mouth, Eloise's lips worked furiously. 'I'm not sure,' she began. 'I don't remember a time I didn't have them. Memories of being punched for taking a toy, or pinched so I didn't complain if we had a fight.'

Harriet frowned. That sounded like the standard behaviour of older siblings, not a delusion.

'Eloise, when you were committed, June was no longer living at home. She was at university in Exeter.'

Eloise nodded slowly.

'If your sister wasn't at home during that time, what visions were you having then?'

'They came on when she visited. She looked at me with such… resentment. She always hated me being around her friends…'

Interesting. 'Was that around the time you first met Grant?'

Eloise sucked in a sharp breath. 'I… well yes, but I was only a kid, really. And I didn't spend any time with him.'

'It's ok Eloise, no one is suggesting anything untoward.' Harriet waited while Eloise calmed.

'He was nice to me,' she ventured. 'Made time to talk to me. Until June found us walking in the garden together and...'

'And?' Harriet prompted.

Eloise swallowed, 'I know now she was just protecting me. All she was ever doing was protecting me. That's all she has ever done. I was the one who overreacted. I'm so lucky to have her as my sister. To take care of me, and of... my son.'

Her face crumpled, tears welling in her eyes. Harriet sat back. *Enough*, she thought. Whatever past tensions may have been between the sisters had clearly been healed. June showed no sign of resentment over her sisters delusions, in fact, she seemed most protective of Eloise. If you ignored her affair with Grant of course. There was no advantage to pressing this line of questioning. Anything she needed to know about Eloise's time in Hollydale, she could get from Doctor Taylor.

Shifting the focus to something positive Harriet asked, 'How is Jacob?'

Eloise focus blurred, eyes far away. 'Beautiful,' she said. 'June says he is getting big, two teeth! And he's still sleeping wonderfully, he's such a good little man.'

'When will June bring Jacob for his next visit?'

Her face fell, the tears that had been receding swelled again and breeched Eloise's eyes. She lowered her head, quickly brushing them away. 'It's a long way for Jacob to travel. He's so little. June's right, visits aren't good for him. It would be selfish.'

Harriet felt her brows bunch. No visits? That must weigh on Eloise terribly.

She tried a gentle tack, 'She seems very committed to Jacob, a wonderful aunt.'

Eloise pursed her lips tightly, frustration flashing across her face. She turned her face to the window, the bright lights washing the definition of her face away. Harriet cursed herself. It must be so hard to be away from her child, Harriet couldn't imagine the strain of that separation. She'd meant her comment as encouragement, but could see how it might only serve to remind Eloise that it was her sister caring for her child, not his mother who sat in The Orchard miles away. However much she was thankful to her sibling, that knowledge would still hurt.

Harriet shuffled her papers, giving Eloise a moment to recover.

'I wanted to talk with you about Mr Huxley's custody application, for sole custody of Jacob. When we first spoke you didn't seem aware of it. In the transcript of your police interview it's clear you became very upset when you were shown the document. Can you walk me through that?'

Eloise squeezed her eyes shut. Her hands trembled. Visibly gathering herself she began, 'It was just a shock, I guess. Seeing that letter from the courts. I'd thought things between Grant and I were healing. He took Jacob and me out for lunches, we enjoyed walks on the beach. Only the week before he mentioned taking some time off work to come and stay in Torcross, with me. With us. Though Grant does like to have things his way.' She stopped abruptly, hunching down.

'What do you mean by that?'

'Nothing, it's nothing.' She waved a hand dismissively. Harriet was unconvinced.

'Eloise, what aren't you saying?' Harriet pressed.

Eloise looked up, eyes wide with fear. 'It's just, well, Grant knows how he likes things... it's best to do as he says.'

She looked away, body tense and closed. Harriet knew she would get no more out of her. She filed the comment away for later and continued.

'Returning to the letter, Grant hadn't spoken to you of his custody intentions?'

'No,' Eloise exclaimed, heat coming into her normally calm voice. Harriet looked up. Eloise shook her head. 'No,' calmer now, 'he hadn't mentioned it. And I hadn't seen the letter until that day in the police station...'

'They say you flew into a rage.'

'Did I? I don't remember it that way. Only being very upset. It was a shock. A threat like that to my child. To have him taken away from me...'

'Eloise, are you sure you hadn't seen the letter before?'

'No, never.'

'You didn't come across it when you were looking for your scissors, after June left? Become enraged? Decide to take matters into your own hands with Grant?'

Eloise had gone pale at the mere suggestion. Yet again Harriet wondered just how well she understood that she was facing trial for murder.

Did she just not remember? Or was June lying? Instinctively, Harriet just didn't trust the elder Lane sister.

'I…' Eloise swallowed, 'No. All I remember is looking for my scissors… and then June screaming. I…' she looked up at Harriet, eyes full of tears. 'Do you think that's why I did it? Because of the letter?'

Harriet pressed her lips together, 'It's the motivation the prosecution has put forward. And with your reaction to the letter in questioning…'

'Oh,' Eloise looked around, bewildered. 'I just, I just don't remember. Why can't I remember?'

Her breathing became ragged, her eyes scanning violently side to side.

'Take a deep breath Mrs Lane-Huxley,' Harriet said firmly, 'Eloise, breathe!'

Eloise crashed to the floor, shaking and hyperventilating.

'How could I do it? How could I do it?' she wailed, smacking the flat of her palm against her head and chest. Her nurse, Amelia, crossed the room to her, coming to her side just as Eloise vomited all over the floor. Amelia glanced up at Harriet, her expression an apology. Another nurse entered and between them they half carried, half walked a weeping Eloise from the interview room.

Harriet stood alone in the room, stunned, the acrid stench of sick assailing her nose. She covered her mouth and nose to block the smell and, taking shallow breaths to stave off a sympathy vomit, gathered up her folders.

'Ms Bell?' a deep voice sounded behind her.

Harriet looked around and saw Doctor Taylor standing in the doorway. Tall and lean, dressed in a grey, tailored suit that matched his tired eyes, he looked wrung out but sophisticated.

'Shall we go to my office?' he offered, turning to lead the way.

Thankful to get out of the stinking room, Harriet swiftly followed.

Doctor Taylor took a seat behind his desk and gestured to a chair for Harriet. She perched on the hard wooden stool and waited.

'Panic attack,' he stated simply.

'Are they dangerous? To her health I mean.'

'No, no. Panic attacks may look and feel very scary, but they are just a physical manifestation of fear. Or in Mrs Lane-Huxley's case, trauma. They happen most often when she is talking about the events of November 15th, when she is pushed to remember.

'So this wasn't the first time?'

'No it was not. In fact, for Eloise the attacks have been becoming more regular. Though the valium seems to be helping.'

Harriet nodded, gathering herself.

'Can I ask you a few questions Doctor Taylor? Seeing as I am here?'

'Of course Ms Bell. What would you like to know?'

Harriet shuffled through her folder producing a neat white sheet. 'I have a copy of your report on Eloise, from the DPP.'

'Naturally,' Doctor Taylor replied.

'You state she is doing better, improving. But just now you told me her panic attacks are becoming more frequent.'

'Panic attacks are not always a sign of a deterioration of mental illness, Ms Bell. They can be symptom of the mind healing. Remembering.'

'And is she? Remembering?'

Doctor Taylor sighed deeply, slouching back in his chair and adjusting his silver-framed glasses. 'Not as we would like, no. Details of her life and memories, are all sharp and defined. But events surrounding her husband's death… she has remembered no more than you already know, flashes of her sister covered in blood, the scissors on the bathroom floor. Nothing of Beesands or Grant Huxley. At least, nothing she has admitted.'

Harriet narrowed her eyes at the doctor. 'That's a leading thing to say Doctor Taylor. You could be read to be implying…'

'I imply nothing,' Doctor Taylor held up his hands in submission.

'Do you think she remembers more than she is letting on?' Harriet pushed.

Doctor Taylor paused, 'I have worked here many years Ms Bell. Most of my patients are, to put it mildly, unpleasant.'

Try defending a rapist, Harriet thought. Then considered he probably treated the insane ones and suppressed a shudder.

Doctor Taylor continued, 'Eloise is different. Open, eager even, to participate in treatment. I can't help but think how differently this all could have worked out had she sought treatment before things got to this point. Of course, I understand her reluctance, her past experiences at Hollydale were not, positive. Few people who experience electroshock therapy are keen to try it again anytime soon.'

'But do you think she is lying?'

He fixed Harriet with his eyes, 'No, Ms Bell. I do not. I find Mrs Lane-Huxley to be sincere. Coupled with her previous history of delusion and treatment as a teenager, I believe this episode of amnesia to be genuine.'

Harriet allowed herself to let out a heavy breath and relaxed her shoulders. 'So her memory is sound. But just not at that moment?'

Doctor Taylor nodded.

'Doesn't fit well with the criminal definition of insanity then,' Harriet continued. As she had suspected. Automatism was definitely the right direction for her defence.

'No,' Dr Taylor agreed. 'But I don't believe she was in her right mind, or even in control of her mind when Mr Huxley met his fate.'

'A temporary disease of the mind?'

'Would be my clinical opinion, yes.'

'Brought on by extreme stress? Like the threat to her child?'

'Protecting one's young is a base instinct in all of us. For someone with Eloise's fragile mental health, to discover such a threat could reasonably trigger an episode of amnesia as she is experiencing.'

'So in your professional opinion, finding the application for custody whilst alone in the house with no one to support her to calm, she could have entered a fugue state?

'Yes.'

'She left the house, her child. Went for her regular walk....'

'Her regular walk you say?'

'Eloise told me that Thursdays she usually went for a walk and June watched over Jacob. But that week June was in Salcombe.'

'So a change in routine and a trigger. Then reverting to her usual routine.'

'Meaning she could conceivably have been going for her regular walk? Following routine rather than acting out a pre-determined plan?'

'That would fit with expected behavioural patterns. How that works for your defence, I can't help you there.'

Harriet met his eyes confidently, 'That's my job, Doctor Taylor.'

Memories of her sister covered in blood were inducing panic attacks, no other recollection of the events of November 15. *How can someone so gentle transform into someone so violent, even for a moment?* Harriet wondered. Despite Randell Dawes' experience of his wife's mental illness, a change so drastic just didn't fit with the Eloise she knew.

Her recollection of her previous committal to Hollydale was fuzzy at best. She recounted the normal childhood torments siblings suffered at the hands of their older siblings. Even Nellie had been known to boss Harriet around from time to time... None of that could be classified as a 'delusion'. There had to be more to that story.

June remained a confusing character. So protective of Eloise, yet she had had an affair with Grant. Such a deep betrayal. And now, deciding it best not to bring Jacob to visit? The justification seemed legitimate, on the surface. But to keep a child from his mother? Eloise saw only love in her sister's actions. Perhaps Harriet was over thinking it. She hadn't warmed to June Lane.

What was concerning was Eloise's comment that Grant liked things his way... the flash of fear that filled her eyes, what wasn't she saying? Had Grant been controlling, or worse, abusive? June hadn't thought so. But what do we really know of the relationships of others? She'd have to see if she could get more out of Eloise about that.

Despite what she was accused of, Harriet's heart went out to the woman, so consumed with guilt over actions she couldn't even recall taking. Eloise had loved her husband, honestly it seemed. And he had let her down, badly. He was going to betray her. *Just like my father*, she thought angrily. But did betrayal justify murder? It certainly explained it.

Harriet shook her head and climbed into her Mazda. Doctor Taylor had given her much to think on, and all but confirmed her and Randell's direction to plead automatism was the correct course. She had to shake off this doubt and focus. Eloise deserved the chance to be treated and heal, to live a life free of illness. She'd never get that chance in prison. No, Harriet had to make sure their defence was solid, and that Eloise was found not guilty due to automatism. Her future depended on it.

Eloise sat on her small cot, the walls of her private room close around her. Legs crossed like a primary school child, she rocked herself gently back and forth, back and forth, arms wrapped about herself. The screams of another patient, probably Maddie Hall, the child-killer, echoed down the hall outside. Eloise pressed her eyes shut and tried to focus on her breathing. *Slow, steady, calm. Think of a river, place your fears on a leaf and watch the currents carry them away. Slow, steady calm.*

She repeated the mantra until the trembling of her limbs began to still.

She'd got worked up again. It didn't matter what she said to herself once she got into that state, she couldn't stop it. The pent up energy would build and build until it burst like a damn through her chest, cascading through her body, carrying her with it. After, it took time to calm down. Discipline. Routine. Control. She had to regain that if she ever wanted to get out of here.

A surge of panic gripped her in an iron and unforgiving fist. Breathing out heavily she released her arms and stretched out on her back, eyes to the ceiling. This place was so suffocating. Small rooms, long corridors, soft pink couches, pale blue nurses. Beige and plain and tight.

She hated it, but it was still the better option. If she wanted to ensure she was never sent back to Hollydale, she had to follow the rules, control her emotions. Anywhere was better than Hollydale.

How did she ever end up here?

In her mind she pictured her home in Torcross. The open rooms, the cream furniture, the large windows facing the lake that lined the sea. Jacob playing with brightly coloured blocks on an alphabet rug.

Jacob.

She rolled onto her side and squeezed the bridge of her nose. Harriet was a good person. She was working hard, trying to help her. Honestly trying. It was nice, to have someone in her corner, for once in her life. Eloise released a sigh. *Everyone should have a friend like Harriet,* she thought. *She makes you believe in yourself, even if you shouldn't.* She glanced over at the small photo pinned to her wall. Dark smiling eyes, gummy grin, shining golden curls. She kissed her finger tips and pressed them to the photo of Jacob, tears in her eyes.

'I'm coming home, baby,' she whispered to the colourless walls. 'Somehow, I'm coming home.'

13: The past won't rest

Harriet shut and locked her apartment door, while simultaneously kicking off her high heels. It had been a long day going into London and now she wanted nothing more than a glass of wine and the leftover pizza in her fridge. Maybe she'd read a few chapters of Kate Atkinson's Case Histories, and then bed...

She was padding down her hallway, pulling her jacket from her shoulders when she heard voices. Music blared and she realised the sound was coming from her TV. She strode across her lounge and flicked off the box. *Strange*, she thought to herself, *I don't remember turning that on this morning*. Dismissing the mystery with a quick shrug, Harriet strolled into her kitchen and opened her fridge door.

'Hey there stranger!' called a loud booming voice. Harriet nearly leaped from her skin. Snapping her head in the direction of the voice she froze in surprise. At the door to her kitchen, head thrown back, laughter erupting from his mouth, was Billy.

'Oh Hare!' he grinned, wiping the mirth from his eyes, 'you should'a seen your face.'

Harriet let out a frustrated breath, heart beat lowering rapidly from the extreme level it had ratcheted up to when she'd heard that unexpected call. Embarrassment, dressed as anger replacing her fear.

'What the fuck Billy?' she exclaimed, pulling the wine from the fridge. 'How the hell'd you get in here?'

Billy held up set of keys dangling from a worn blue key ring, 'You never changed the locks. They say you should do that. After a break up.'

Harriet kicked the fridge door shut and, snatching up a glass, stalked passed her brother and into the lounge.

'You can't break up with family,' she hissed.

'Yeah, and that still shits you hey?' he returned.

Harriet glared at him and flopped down on her couch, stretching out her legs, blocking Billy from sitting down.

He smirked at her and perched on the arm of the lounge.

'What are you doing here anyway?' Harriet demanded, taking a gulp of her wine.

'Can't a brother come and visit his big sister?'

'No. Not without a phone call first, he can't. Besides, it's mid-week. You have work tomorrow...'

Billy shrugged, 'Took some leave.'

Harriet narrowed her eyes at him, 'It's a new job Billy. What leave?'

Billy looked away, eyeing the apartment. 'Hasn't changed a bit,' he said, lifting up her feet and plonking himself on the sofa. Harriet wriggled up, grudgingly making room for him beside her.

'It's changed a lot thank you. Much cleaner.'

Billy grinned at her, before reaching over and taking her glass. Taking a deep drink before returning the wine, he glanced at her askance.

'Crystal kicked me out,' he said.

'What? When? And more importantly *why*?'

Billy smiled ruefully, eyes avoiding hers, 'Last night. Caught me toking. Bad for the baby, apparently.'

Harriet sat up straight, pulling her legs in under herself to create some height. 'Apparently? Well no shit Billy. What were you thinking?'

He shrugged, 'I was bored.'

'And what about the garage? You didn't get fired again did you?'

'No, no. I'm not lying, Hare. Dave gave me some time off. Unpaid leave. Works a bit slow for him, so...'

'So not fired, but not working either.'

'It's temporary.'

Harriet scoffed, rolling her eyes. 'And you are here because?'

'I just thought it's been a while since we caught up...'

'You don't want mum and dad to know, right?'

He looked at her sheepishly, 'Right.'

Harriet sighed heavily and refilled her glass.

'Billy,' Harriet said, voice stern. 'You need to fix things with Crystal. Running down here isn't going to help anything, and with the baby...'

'I know, I know... I just need a bit of time out, you know?'

Harriet frowned and reached for the TV remote, flicking on the news. They sat in silence a moment, feigning interest in the February weather forecast. Grey, cloudy, sunny spells. Nothing noteworthy.

'So,' Billy ventured, 'can I stay? You know, for a bit?'

Harriet paused, assessing him over the rim of her wine glass. She sighed heavily. 'Of course you can stay. But I'm not cleaning up after you, not like before. And I don't cook for two, so it's take away or chef Bill. Got it?'

'Indian or Thai?' Billy asked, pulling his phone from his pocket.

'Thai,' Harriet smiled. As Billy punched in the Deliveroo search, she heaved herself from the couch and returned to the kitchen, collected up another wine glass from the kitchen and filled it for Billy.

Returning to the lounge she handed it to him, 'You gotta fucking grow up Bill.'

'Yeah,' Billy said, hand rubbing his short cropped hair, 'I know.'

The TV light cast a cool blue glow across the lounge as Harriet sat reading client files at her dinning table. Rolling her stiff shoulders she glanced over at her brother. In the soft light she could just make out the back of his head tucked into a groove on the lounge arm, one hand dangling before him. *I bet you're asleep,* she thought as she stood and walked across the room. Eyes closed, breathing heavy, Billy looked peaceful, calm, in a way he rarely did in the light of day. Harriet sighed, gathering up a blanket and laying it over her wayward brother before making her way to bed and rest. She left the TV on, its soft voices filling the space around Billy, to keep him company.

'Morning.'

Harriet looked up from her files and took another sip of coffee. 'Sleep ok?' she asked.

Billy nodded and padded into the kitchen. He emerged with his own steaming cup of bitter morning kick-starter. Harriet slurped down the last of her own and stood up, gathering folders into her bag.

'You going in already?' Billy asked, surprised. 'I thought you lawyers got to sleep in.'

Harriet pressed her lips together, determined not to bite back.

'I have a client meeting at 10 a.m. over at Longhorn Correctional and reams of notes still to review. I work better in my office.'

'Good to know the wicked are up at the same time as us hard working folks.' Billy quipped.

'At least us "wicked types" earn our own keep,' she snapped.

'Honest work never pays. Keeps us little guys down.'

Harriet saw red. The long hours, the lack of sleep, the rapist she had to meet with this morning, the weird uncertainty she felt about Eloise's case, all her challenges reared up before her and found a focus for release: Billy Bell.

'You chose to be a "little guy" Billy. You had a way out.'

'A factory worker's son from Ellesmere Port? Bullshit, Hare.'

'You did and you threw it away. And you fucking know it Billy. Do you remember what I promised you that summer after Nellie died? When dad left the first time and mum fell apart? I promised I would never leave you. That I would wait for you and we would go together. Remember that?' Harriet paused, eyes burning into Billy's now somber face.

'I waited for you,' she continued. 'Two fucking years longer in Ellesmere working a Tesco checkout to save up enough for us to come down here to uni. And you made it. You got your grades and we left. You and me, we got out. And then what happened, huh Billy? What happened then?'

'Fuck off, Hare.'

'Fuck off? Fuck off!' Harriet stormed up to her brother and shoved her face up to his, expression menacing. 'You got on fucking crack. Lost your scholarship. Nearly fucking died. And you gave it all up.'

Reciprocal anger flared across Billy's face. 'I got off that shit. And you know it. I worked fucking hard and I got clean.'

'And then you went back north. Back to the factory and the 'honest life' that holds you down so much. Under the boot of us 'uni types'. You chose that life. I. GOT. YOU. OUT. You went back. That shit's on you.'

'Just 'coz I don't have a degree doesn't make me dad.'

'Tell that to Crystal!'

The anger faded from Billy's eyes and he looked down at his hands, something like shame flickering across his features. Huffing in exasperation, Harriet went to the kitchen, slammed her dirty mug down on the sink and stormed out. Collecting up her satchel she made for the door.

Billy's voice stopped her, 'You ever think maybe the drugs weren't the problem, Hare? Might've just been the symptom?'

Harriet whirled around to face her brother. But Billy's eyes remained downcast. 'This,' he gestured to the apartment, taking in the city beyond, 'it's nice. But it's not for everyone.' He held his hands out before him, palms up in supplication. 'Not everyone can live in their head.' He tapped his temple.

'You have the brains Billy, that's a cop out.'

Billy nodded, finally looking up at her. Face solemn. 'Doesn't mean its right for me. A life like this. You thrive here, in the inner city. Popping into London and other powerful places, all dressed up in your fancy suits. Trips out to nice restaurants, the theatre.'

'I work fucking hard, Billy. It's not a cake walk.'

'I know,' he said quietly, 'I know you do. And I could never do it, Hare. It wasn't the drugs, or bad friends. It was me. And it killed me that you didn't see, didn't understand… me.'

Harriet stared at her brother, mouth open in surprise. She snapped it shut and straightened her back. 'Wash the dishes,' she said and walked out the door.

14: Nellie Bell

Fucking Danny Flint. Short and stocky, weathered and greying, tattoo of a skull along his temple, shaved head and all the arrogance of a god damned prince.

Flint leaned back in his metal chair, stretching the chains of his cuffs to their full extent. He grinned appreciatively at Harriet, missing front tooth on open display. She didn't meet the languid sweep of his eyes as they made their way up and down her body.

She sat up straighter, worked to keep her face neutral. Danny rolled his tongue slowly over his lips. He could at least *try* not to act like a fucking predator. Harriet felt dirty, disgusted and ready to just give up. Danny Flint didn't need a lawyer, he needed a deep, deep grave.

'Mr Flint, this is not your first charge of assault. You have served time,' she consulted her notes, 'twice. Once on Detention and Training Order as you were 16 at the time of the crime and once for seven years, in your 40s. A judge would look favourably on a guilty plea, and a show of remorse.'

'Can't show remorse for something I never dun.' His eyes glowed, daring Harriet to challenge him.

'Mr Flint, it is my job as your lawyer to ensure you are appraised of the whole situation and to advise you of the most appropriate course of action. On the facts, I advise you to plead guilty. It would still mean time in prison, but your cooperation would mean a reduction in sentence. This is your last chance to consider a change of plea.'

Flint's face morphed into a look of fake surprise and disappointment, 'Am I to believe,' he crooned, 'my own lawyer doesn't even believe me?' Suddenly he shot forward, arms slamming down on the table between them, metal ringing off metal, Flint's body straining to close the distance between them.

To her annoyance, the sudden movement caught her off guard and Harriet gave a quick jerk backward. Flint grinned darkly, face close enough that she could smell his stale breath. The man needed a good dentist.

A guard stepped forward, eyebrows raised at Harriet in question. She gave a small nod. They were done here.

'Okay, I accept your instructions to plead not guilty Mr Flint notwithstanding my advice and we will enter that plea of not guilty at your arraignment next week.' She commenced collecting her notes swiftly, 'If anything else comes to mind regarding the night of January 3, anything at all to give you an alibi, please contact my office.'

Flint smirked, settling back down onto his seat. 'Already told ya everything missy. I was at the pub, but I never touched that bitch Malley. I don't do dykes.'

Harriet, face turned towards her satchel, glanced heavenward. *Give me strength*, she breathed. Malley Tucker was an 18 year old student at Exeter University, studying graphic design. 'Girls night out gone wrong: Britains drinking problem putting young women at risk,' the tabloids proclaimed, like somehow she was responsible for her own assault. How dare a woman leave the house and have fun? Bastard papers. On the night of the assault she'd had long blonde hair and a ready smile. Now, courtesy of Danny fucking Flint, she had another two operations remaining to finish the reconstruction of a smashed cheek bone and a lifetime of psychological treatment for trauma to try and claw back some semblance of normalcy in her life. She'd cut off her hair since - shaved it to her scalp. He'd used it to hold her down…

'Perhaps work on a different way of expressing that before we go to trial, Mr Flint. Miss Tucker is a person, and should be treated as such.'

'Dyke's a dyke.'

She wanted to puke.

'I'll see you Thursday, Mr Flint,' she said and strode out, her back crawling from the possessive stare she knew followed her exit.

An involuntary shiver coursed down her spine as Harriet stood in the Exeter Magistrates Court. From the dock, Danny Flint's sly eyes scanned up and down Harriet's body like an unwanted caress. *Arrogant prick*, she thought. Taking a deep breath she returned her attention to gathering her files.

Plea entered: Not Guilty

Utter bullshit, he did it for sure. But it wasn't Harriet's job to prove that. Thankfully, in this case at least, the DPP seemed to be on the ball. Two officers arrived to escort Danny to the van that would return him to Langhorn Correctional; no bail for this repeat offender. Harriet strode from the courtroom, suppressing a shudder at the thought of Flint on the streets. His hagged, drawn visage, smoke-stained teeth and macho grin. Those eyes. Harriet took pride in doing a tough job well, but maybe she'd do it just a little less well in this case.

She broke free of the court room and into the frosty February air. The cold slap oddly welcome on her hot skin; flushed from the tension of remaining neutral in the face of Danny's cold stare.

The bane of all defence lawyers: the obviously guilty. And for Harriet in particular: rapists. Foul scum.

Striding across the carpark, a familiar figure caught her eye as he walked along the far side of the asphalt. DS Robert Fields raised a hand in greeting and closed the space between them. The tension of the courtroom morphed into an odd bubble of anticipation in her gut. She'd enjoyed their banter at the pub a few weeks ago. Time for round two?

Pulling herself up to her full, albeit unimpressive height, Harriet plastered a cocky grin on her face and waited. Robert stopped a few steps from her side and smiled.

'Court date?' he asked.

'Arraignment. Trial date set for March 1st. You?'

'Just checking in on a DI. You might have seen it in the papers. We nabbed bloody Danny Flint. Wanted to check all went well with the plea. Can you believe the idiot plead not guilty? No jury in the country is going to go for that!'

His eyes shone with frustrated mirth.

Harriet shifted uncomfortably.

Robert's eyes narrowed, then widened in realisation. 'Oh shit, he's yours isn't he? I didn't mean…'

Harriet held up a hand, 'It's all right. I'm just following my client's instructions.'

Robert eyed her. 'You know he's got priors right? Like a list a mile long…' He stopped himself, realising what he was saying. Harriet stared at him, incredulous. Of course she knew his history. *Geez Robert, think before you open your god damned mouth.*

'Sorry,' he said.

'Like I said, I'm following my client's instructions. Everyone deserves a defence.' The line rolled off her tongue, oddly flat and meaningless in the light of Danny Flint's reputation.

She tried to rally, to find a bit of pep and change the subject. But her words had dried up.

Robert scanned her face. 'Wanna grab a coffee?' he asked.

Harriet hesitated. It was a bad idea. He was the opposition on the Lane-Huxley case. He was a good 15 years her senior. He was also ridiculously good looking, even in the grey sunshine of Exeter in winter.

She cocked her head and hitched up the corner of her mouth. 'Think I can find the time,' she replied, eyebrow arched in invitation.

Robert's dark eyes glimmered in the sun. 'Right,' he stammered, suddenly unsure.

Good, she'd unsettled him. Much better.

'Come on,' she said, taking the lead. 'I know a reasonable place just down the road.'

Seated across from each other in the Corner Cuppa cafe, Robert watched as Harriet wrapped her frozen fingers elegantly around her latte and sipped the milky liquid. His eyes dipped to her lips as she licked a bubble of froth from the corner of her mouth, watched her settling her cup on its saucer. Catching himself, he hoped she didn't notice. She flicked her ponytail over her shoulder and glanced about the room, giving Robert a moment to collect his focus. A small smile on her lips. Yep, she noticed.

'So,' he began. 'Been out dancing at the Red Lion lately?'

Harriet nearly snorted her coffee as the unexpected tack caught her by surprise. She swallowed her sip and eyed Robert over her mug. 'Need a dance partner?'

'Me?' he feigned innocence, 'Oh no. Asking for a friend.'

'Come now,' Harriet crooned, 'I promise I'd make you look good.'

'That, I believe,' he said leaning forward, eyes suddenly serious, intense.

Harriet sat up straighter, ignoring the shift in tone between them. She shuffled on her seat, uncomfortable. 'So, are you going to tell me then,' she began, working back towards safer ground. 'What made you become a cop?'

She expected him to laugh, he could see it in her eyes. Such a cliché question. He must be sick of answering it. But instead Robert turned his gaze inward, reflective. Harriet watched his focus deepen, eyebrows drawing down. She twitched, waiting.

'Well,' Robert said, nodding slowly, tone ominous, 'if I really think about it… it was probably because of my dad.'

He paused. Watched as Harriet leaned forward, drawn subconsciously towards the horror she expected he was about to share. He suppressed the smile hovering behind his lips. 'He was a cop,' Robert continued. 'Grandfather was a cop. Mum and grandma, the wives of cops…'

Harriet tipped back her head and laughed out loud. Robert grinned.

'I had you going, didn't I?'

She wiped a tear of mirth from her eye. 'So your kids are gonna be cops too, then?' she said through her laughter.

'Tom? After he finishes his career at Arsenal, undoubtedly,' Robert said.

Harriet pulled a face. 'Arsenal? Uck, lad can do better than that!'

'Yeah, yeah. You're from the north right? I can't quite pick the accent but I'm gonna guess Liverpool?'

'You'll never walk alone!' Harriet cried, eyes gleaming. 'Geez, if I had a pound for every time my dad sung that when I was growing up…'

Robert grinned and they shared a quiet moment of amusement.

Draining his cup, Robert leaned back. 'So what about you? Why the law?'

'Aside from my life goal to be a thorn in the side of all cops?' Harriet quipped, lips curved in a seductive smirk, 'I believe in justice. I'll play the game of course, but ultimately justice is what I want to find. Give everyone a voice, a chance.'

'A noble goal. And one we share, whether or not you believe it.'

'I believe it. I might work the other side of cases to you, but that doesn't mean I don't see that you try. I've seen that first hand.'

She turned away, as if uncomfortable delivering the compliment, looking out the window to the street outside. A stiff wind was whipping through the trees, scattering litter and billowing the skirts of the unwary.

'Sound like there's a story there,' Robert prompted.

Harriet blinked slowly. He watched the indecision work its way across her face. He thought he'd lost her, then, 'My sister, Nellie was her name, was murdered when she was 16. Found beaten to death in an alleyway.'

Shocked, Robert gaped a moment. And he'd played that stupid joke about his dad… 'Shit, Harriet. I'm sorry…'

Harriet shook her head, swelling a gulp of coffee. 'Don't be,'she said. 'It was a long time ago. And I think I've spent enough time ignoring that she existed. But she did exist. I had an older sister. And she was pretty damn awesome.'

Robert smiled gently. He knew when to stay silent.

Harriet continued, 'She was five years older than me. So I guess she was kinda my hero, you know? Tall, well for my family anyway. She took after dad, always doing something exciting. She was all I wanted to be back then. Went out one night with her boyfriend, Tyler Marks. Didn't come home.'

Harriet paused, hands now gripping her latte like a lifeline. 'They found her the next morning, behind the Shooters night club. We hadn't even missed her yet.'

'Was it the boyfriend?' Robert asked softly. It almost always was in stories like this.

Harriet shrugged. 'Couldn't prove it. They were out together. Were seen making out in the alley. He said he left her there to "clean up after," such a gentleman,' Harriet snorted. 'He went back to a mate's place that night. Said she never came back inside. That he figured she'd gone home.'

'He didn't look for her?'

Harriet's eyebrows shrugged ruefully for her. 'There was no DNA to connect him to the crime. Well, no blood. Plenty of other DNA, but that fit with his story. So…'

'So, no case?'

'Yep. At best he was an inconsiderate arsehole who didn't check on her. At worst…'

Robert frowned in mutual understanding, nodding to himself. 'I've seen my fair share of cases like that. They don't ever let you go.'

'Some do get under your skin, don't they?' Harriet said. 'I never thought they would, after Nellie. Thought she was my one for life, you know?'

He did. What a story. And the irony of it, to end up defending a piece of shit like bloody Danny Flint. *Fuck.*

'So why defence?' he asked, 'I'd have thought an experience like that would lead to the DPP?'

'Yeah, well, you can thank my brother Billy for that. He was only 11 when Nellie died. Mum fell apart, dad hit the bottle and left. So for a while there it was really just Billy and me. We got ourselves through it all.

'Mum and dad reconciled about a year later, but Billy never really felt he had a father after that.'

Robert watched her face, seeing what she didn't say written clearly over her skin. *Not just Billy*, he suspected.

'Bill lost his way a bit when he moved to Exeter for uni, got in with the wrong crowd. Got himself arrested for selling dope. Just 18. Bloody idiot. Did time. Only a few months, but prison is prison. It was just wrong. Prison should be a last resort. People make mistakes, especially young idiots from lower socioeconomic families. It wasn't right.'

'Not justice.'

'Not justice,' she agreed. 'I had to pick which one to fight for: justice for Nellie or justice for Billy. Bill's still here, I guess. Though it sometimes feels like I chose the wrong sibling.' She huffed a laugh. Their eyes locked, Robert held her stare. Moments passed.

'So how's he doing now? Your brother?'

Harriet blew out a heavy sigh, 'Having a baby with his girlfriend, but living in my apartment.'

'Well, there's good and unexpected there.'

Harriet laughed, light returning to her eyes, 'Good and unexpected. Yeah, I reckon you've got Billy in one there.' She smiled to herself. Robert could see it, swimming under the surface of the mask. The pain and hurt, the intense and honest love. Billy was a lucky man to have a sister like Harriet.

She looked up, suddenly contemplative, 'How do you know?' she asked.

'Know what?'

'Who to believe? When you are interviewing suspects, how do you know who to trust?'

Robert paused, giving the question the gravitas it deserved. 'You look at the facts. Work the timelines. The truth is usually pretty obvious from that.'

Harriet rolled her eyes and groaned, 'Yes, yes, facts. I know. Facts are 'king'. But how do you *know*.' She emphasised the word, a hand gesturing to her gut. Robert knew exactly what she meant. That bubble that formed, the confidence that gripped you, shook you and wouldn't let go. Instinct.

'Yes,' he acknowledged her pointing hand with a flick of his eye, 'it's a feeling. Sometimes you just get a sense and you know. But mostly, it's in their eyes.'

Harriet watched him intensely. 'Their eyes.' It wasn't a question, but he answered it.

'Yes, you can see it. The truth, the lies. It's just there.'

She nodded slowly the glow of curiosity fading from her features. 'I guess you and I just read eyes differently, then,' she said, voice suddenly tight. Tension stretched the skin of her face over her bones.

The warmth of connection that had been building between them instantly cooled. Her comment evoking the unspoken block that sat between them. The Lane-Huxley case, or as Harriet had suggested when they last spoke, Lane vs Lane-Huxley. Sister's word against sister. Dangerous ground. Was she really doubting her client's guilt? Or was this just part of the game?

'I've been doing this a long time, Harriet,' Robert hedged, 'It's easy to be drawn into a story...'

She cut him off, 'A lot of people have been telling me that lately. But that's not what I am doing. Regardless, I don't think we have the whole 'story' yet either way.'

'Harriet, we shouldn't...'

'... Talk about the case, I know. And the day is getting on. I should get back to the office.'

'Yeah, me too,' Robert said, bewildered and defeated. Her mood had shifted so quickly. He hadn't wanted to upset her, to seem rude. But there she was, eyes aflame, because of him. He watched as she rose from her chair, shucked on her jacket and coat. Bundled against the day, and against his belief she turned to leave.

'Say hi to June for me,' she called over her shoulder as she walked out the door.

Margaret Ives stood at her front window watching the wind whip across the lake that sat before the waters of Torcross beach. The sky was darkening, the temperature pushing zero. Across the way she watched as a tall figure clad in a dark jacket pushed a pram around the lake, again.

Every day June walked that route, whatever the weather. It had become like a ritual since all that unpleasantness with Eloise. *Probably doesn't want to even think of Beesands*, Margaret mused, *I don't want to think of Beesands.*

The horrible murder of Grant Huxley had reached into her peaceful little world and exploded a bomb of gossip, rumour and fear. *Selfish girls, both of them*, Margaret thought, *taking a baby out in this weather!*

She shook her head in distaste and pulled the window firmly closed.

Tonight there would be snow, her joints told her so.

March

15: Unexpected evidence

'Breathe in. Hold. Breathe out. Now lower yourself into the stretch. Hold.'

PC Tracy Berry moved with the confident fluidity of practice from downward facing dog, lengthening her hamstrings, into a curl and down, down, down to the floor and cobra pose. Her muscles burned, her lungs heaved, her face was lacquered in sweat. God she loved Hot Yoga.

An hour later, brightly coloured active wear swapped for her modest police uniform, Tracy exited the humid sweat of the Salcombe Health Club. Savouring the crisp bite of the early morning air Tracy mounted her bike and headed for the station. Her route took her down Sowton Park and Ride, the beautiful tree lined lane, ferns reaching out to her through the fading mists, up to Rydon Lane and eventually the Devon and Cornwall Police Station.

The health club was a new thing. Not the fitness, just the method. Tracy, a Yorkshire girl to her bones was born 'well built'. Unlike the other teenagers in her peer group, who focused on diets and skinniness, Tracy had always seen her powerful legs and broad shoulders as an advantage, elected captain of the hockey, netball and tennis teams every year. Rounding a corner she sprung from her bike and walked it up the station drive. Pulling out her bike chain, she tied off her vehicle and headed inside.

'Morning, Trace,' Angela Cummins, the desk clerk waved an age-swollen hand, nails bedecked in purple with silver glitter today.

'Nice nails, Ange,' Tracy smiled as she moved past the front desk and into the office proper.

'I knew you'd like 'em,' Angela called back, a grin breaking out over her face.

'Brilliant,' Tracy replied. Thumbs up. Through the door. Before the eye roll could break through her façade. Tracy liked Angela, a lot. They were of an age. Both called from a life of motherhood and cafe catch ups, back into the office by the shock of divorce. They enjoyed a regular pint and pie at their local pub on a Wednesday evening, conversation and laughter flowing with the beer. Angela was a delight to be around. Her nails on the other hand…

Tracy entered the office, large high-ceilinged, lined with desks and strode to the notice board: nothing new. She placed her lunch: yogurt and fruit, chicken and avocado sandwich (wholemeal of course) and a slice of cheese, in the staff fridge between the milk and leftover birthday cake (Benny turned 25 yesterday), and headed to her desk.

She surveyed her correspondence, all in order. Tracy smiled to herself. It really was beginning to feel normal again, being here, doing this job. Over the last few months, since the Hiddley Drive incident, she'd felt shaky, doubting her choice to return; feeling too old for the drama. But sitting at her desk, the quiet murmurs of the office around her, muscles heavy and warm from yoga, Tracy remembered she could do this. She could do all of this.

'Bloody phone rang off the hook all night,' Benny slumped against her desk. 'More reports of white cars seen around Beesands last November. Like anyone bloody remembers seeing a white car on a specific day 3 months ago!'

Tracy's confidence wavered. Two women, pale-faced, wild eyes… the blood. She shut out the image that sprang up before her. Scissors, blades long and sharp, the white hand reaching down for them…

'Sure they do,' she answered hoping her voice sounded light, nonchalant. 'You see one everyday round here.'

Benny snorted, 'Don't think these public appeals for info really do much other than take up my time…'

Tracy looked at the young man, fatigue sat beneath his eyes. Night shift did suck.

She strengthened her resolve. She could do *all* of it.

'Want a hand with the leads? I could spare an hour…'

'Nah, nah. Thanks though Trace. Ahmed's on it for now. A shop hold up needs follow up though. Thought I could throw that your way?'

Relief flooded through Tracy's limbs. She hoped it didn't show on her face. 'Sure thing boss. What's the address?'

* * *

Hours later Tracy strolled back passed the front desk. Angela glanced up at her surreptitiously.

'All good there, Trace?'

'Yeah, yeah, long day that's all.'

'Wanna grab a bite after work?'

'Sounds good, Ange.' Tracy patted her friend's back as she passed, mind already thinking of a hot cup of tea and her dried apricots. That shopkeeper had been an arrogant pig. Yes, I am here to help you. No that doesn't mean you can blame the entire police force for the break in. Yes, I need to know where you were. No, you aren't a suspect... yet.

She heard the station door open and waved to Ange as she moved for the office.

'Hello,' Ange's bright voice called. 'Can I help?'

Such a former sales girl. Tracy grinned, pushing the door. Then paused. A familiar voice drifted through the office.

'Um, yes. Well, maybe. Actually, no. Thank you, no. I'm fine.'

Tracy turned, striding forward passed Ange's quizzical face and into the foyer.

'Helene?' she called.

The woman was already half way out the door. She turned back. Definitely Helene, Tracy would know those eyes anywhere. Eyes were the key to a good yoga instructor, you had to believe their bullshit about energy and vibes, even if just for the hour you were sweating in their class. Helene's kind but tired face registered Tracy with a brief moment of surprise, then a warm smile.

'Tracy? I didn't realise you worked here,' she said, then shook her head, embarrassed, 'I mean, of course I knew you were a... I've seen the uniform after class... but I never put it together.'

'Not our usual meeting ground,' Tracy replied smoothly.

Helene smiled, stuck in the doorway, frozen.

'So,' Tracy ventured, 'what's up?'

'Oh, it's nothing. I was just listening to the radio and... But, no, honestly I don't want to waste your time.'

Tracey saw the hesitation, the glow of concern in Helene's eyes. She had something to say, but she was unsure.

'Well,' Tracy said, 'I'm actually on a break,' she shot Ange a glance. Ange nodded subtly, she would cover for her. 'How about we grab a coffee? There's a nice little cafe just down the road.'

'I...'

'Be lovely really,' Tracy pushed, 'a chat out of the Health Club. Just you and me. We can talk about anything.'

Tracy read the understanding and gratitude in Helene's eyes. 'If you are sure you have the time?'

'Always.'

Silently Tracey sent thanks to DS Fields. Sometimes someone just needed to talk, out of the office.

Angela's nails clacked on the keyboard. Not long now before end of shift. Oooh, she couldn't wait for a cider. *I hope Tracy isn't much longer*, she thought, eyes flicking to the clock in the bottom right of her computer screen.

As if summoned by thought Tracy stepped through the station door, freezing wind trailing her.

Her face was pale, drawn. She looked defeated.

Instantly Angela was on her feet, face enquiring. Tracy barely glanced her way as she moved through the foyer and came to her side.

'I think I need to ring DS Fields,' she said.

16: The white car

The driveway was empty, Robert noted. June's Land Rover was parked just up the street. He filed that little fact away in his brain. Surprised but welcoming, June led Robert and Anita into her dining-lounge.

'Take a seat at the table. I'll just check on Jacob and I will be with you.'

She bustled across the room and into Jacob's nursery. Presumably the boy was sleeping.

Robert strolled across the room, eyes scanning the photo frames along the wall, the book shelves stuffed full of brightly coloured picture books, the odd teddy-bear or plastic dinosaur crammed between the spines. Idly he ran his finger across the books, *The Hungry Caterpillar, Winnie the Poo, Alice in Wonderland, Grimms' Fairy Tales.* Jacob would be read widely from the classics of childhood literature.

June slipped quietly from Jacob's room and, spying Robert at the book shelf, gifted him a warm smile. 'Ours, Lou and me, from when we were little. Mum kept them all, brought them over when Lou moved in here. Feels special to share our books with him.'

Robert nodded, Thomas' books had all been newly bought, same titles, updated editions. Gemma had insisted. 'Your books were yours. These are Tom's.' The corner of his mouth quirked privately at the memory. She'd been such a protective and assertive mother, glowing with the joy of the new role. Tom all rolls and squeals. The boy had never sat still for a moment, not much had changed there. Robert shook his head, bringing himself out of the memory and into the present. He needed to focus.

'I see you have multiples of several of these,' he said conversationally, indicating the book titles. 'Family presents?'

June pursed her lips. 'Not exactly. Lou wasn't big on sharing when she was little. Didn't like that they'd been mine before. So mum bought her new copies of some of her favourites, like *Peter Rabbit*. Still,' June shrugged, 'means we have a back up now.'

Smiling she made her way to the table and took a seat opposite Anita. Robert stayed at the book shelf, browsing in silence, purposefully, letting the lull in conversation stretch uncomfortably. Anita followed his lead.

'So,' June eventually began, 'I wasn't expecting you today. Was there something in particular that brought you here?' She addressed the question to Robert who remained impassive at the book shelf. Her eyes swung to Anita, sitting calmly at the table, eyes watching.

Unsettled, June shuffled on her seat. Robert waited, watching her from the corner of his eye. She ran a hand through her hair and leaned forward, hands subconsciously tapping on the wooden table. *Now*, he thought.

Turning, he strolled slowly towards the table, unhurriedly taking his seat and settling down, eyes fixed on June.

'Why did you lie to us about taking the bus back to Torcross on the night of Grant Huxley's murder?' Robert stated simply.

June's mouth dropped open in shock, colour draining from her face.

Instantly her hands began to tremble. 'It's not like that... I.' She pressed a hand to her hair again, eyes flicking between Robert and Anita. Neither spoke or moved.

'I was going to take the bus. That was the plan,' June stammered. 'But then the weather came in so blustery and I didn't have my jacket... So I rang Helene. She's a friend from school, we went to Exeter University together too. And I borrowed her car.'

'And drove straight home?'

'Yes, straight home.'

Anita took up the questioning, 'Are you aware, Ms Lane, that a small white car fitting the description of Helene's vehicle was seen outside the Beesand's hotel on the night of Mr Huxley's murder? At the time you said you were on the bus?'

June swallowed, face pale, 'I think I saw something about that on the news...'

Anita paused for one beat, two. 'By my calculations, if you were driving from Salcombe you'd have had plenty of time to make it to the hotel that night and then return home before PC Tracy Berry arrived on the scene.'

June stared, a deer in headlights.

'This breaks your alibi somewhat, June.' Robert prompted.

Her eyes flashed to him. 'You don't think I...? Oh god.' She covered her mouth with her hands, breathing short.

'So, let's start again,' Anita said. 'After dropping your car at Nelson's Garage. What did you do?'

June stared at her wide-eyed. 'I, just like I said to you. I caught the bus. But then the weather came in, so I rang Helene. I got off the bus and went to hers. Borrowed her car.'

'And then?'

'We talked a while. As I said, we're old friends. And then I drove home. Here,' she emphasised. 'I didn't go anywhere near Beesands. Why would I have?'

Robert rolled his shoulders. 'There was no car in the driveway when we arrived on the scene on the night of November 15. Where was the car?'

'Oh, just up the street. I always park on the street. Jacob likes to play in the drive... The Land Rover's out there now.'

That fit with his observation on arrival today. Robert cast his mind back to the night of the 15th. Had he seen a small white car parked there when he and Anita finally made it to the house after dealing with the body at Beesands? Small white cars were so common. He couldn't be sure. He and Anita glanced at each other.

'That still doesn't explain why you told us you took the bus,' Anita said.

June shook her head slightly, eyes pressed closed. 'I made a mistake. I was flustered. I'd just found my sister covered in blood and I've never been taken in for questioning before.' She paused, hands fluttering at her heart, 'The bus was the original plan. I, I just forgot the change in the moment. I was so distracted...'

Distracted seemed more a play from the Eloise Lane-Huxley handbook, rather out of character for June Lane. Then again, trauma could do that to a person. Robert leaned forward, eyes focused on June's face. 'And you didn't drive to Beesands?'

'No!' she exclaimed. 'No, I didn't. I talked a while with Helene and came straight back. I had no reason to go to Beesands.'

Robert rocked back into his chair, 'So, you weren't planning to meet with Mr Huxley? As you had several times over the previous few weeks?'

Horror washed over June's face. Suddenly, she looked 10 years older. 'Oh,' she breathed, tears springing to her eyes, 'how did you find out?'

'Find out what exactly, Ms Lane?' Anita said.

June turned sharply to look at DI Shan, 'About Grant and me. We were...'

'Fucking?' Anita supplied, eyebrow arched, distaste twisting her lips. 'See, what confuses me, Ms Lane,' Anita continued, 'is just how much you seemed to detest Mr Huxley. The anger you displayed when talking about his treatment of your sister and Jacob and his plans for custody. And yet now we find out you were having an affair with him. With your sister's husband.'

June's eyes darkened. 'I do hate him. But I hate myself more. It was a stupid, stupid mistake. One I will never forgive myself for. But I had ended it. The week before. I was not going to see him that night. I was going home to Lou.'

'Interesting timing, wouldn't you say?' Anita prodded.

June blew out a heavy breath. 'Look, I know how bad this sounds. But it's honestly not what you think. Yes, I made a mistake. A huge disgusting mistake. But I didn't kill Grant. I wasn't there.'

'You came straight home,' Anita repeated.

'Exactly. Look, I've been a terrible, horrible sister. I betrayed Lou. But I couldn't keep up the lie. So I put a stop to it. To the relationship. I didn't kill him.' Wild-eyed she scanned their faces, breath coming shorter and shorter. 'I wasn't there,' she repeated desperately.

Robert relented, they had pushed her enough. 'We know that June,' he said softly. Anita flicked him a quizzical glance. 'We checked the car, no DNA evidence to link it, or you, to the crime scene. Eloise was seen in Beesands *and* returning home that night with blood on her jacket. Her prints are on the murder weapon, Grant's blood on her clothes.' He paused, watching June's face work through emotions of fear, confusion, hope. 'There are millions of little white cars in Britain. White is the most popular colour of new car. The witness didn't get the make or plates and there is no CCTV. From your testimony and Helene's it's doubtful you could have made it to Beesands in time anyway.'

June's breathing calmed, she clenched her hands into fists, 'I wasn't there,' she whispered.

Robert nodded, 'This new information doesn't change our view of the case. But June, 'he fixed her with his eyes, 'details like this? They matter. Your testimony has to be rock solid.'

'I just forgot, I was so flustered...'

'Even so, we can't have missed details like this. Not when we go to court.'

June breathed out, 'She's my sister, DS Fields. I'm on her side.'

'"Her side", June, is proper treatment in a secure facility. "Her side" is safety for herself and for her son Jacob. I understand sibling loyalty. But it is also your responsibility to protect your nephew, is it not?'

Face stunned as though she'd been slapped, June nodded slowly, tears spilling over onto her cheeks. 'Yes, yes of course you're right' she whispered. 'Thank you, Robert.' She looked up at him, solemn, thankful and entirely too full of blind trust.

Robert shifted uneasily.

'Alright then. So, we will adjust your testimony accordingly and move forward. But June, ' he leaned forward, 'no more surprises. Okay?'

June nodded, numb.

Robert and Anita rose. 'We will leave you now. Please think back through your statement. Someone will be in touch soon to make a time for you to come to the station and revise the details to reflect the night more accurately.'

'Okay,' June murmured eyes downcast.

'We'll see ourselves out.'

'Wait! Please, please don't tell my family about me and Grant. It's… everything is just so terrible already.'

'We will do our best to keep it private, it's not important to our case. But, I can't speak for the defence and how they may wish to use this information. It may be worth making time to speak with all concerned, privately.'

June nodded, eyes going distant. 'Thank you anyway,' she said.

Robert stood on the street outside June's home and looked down towards the beach. He could hear the crashing waves, smell the salty air. Pale sunlight kissed his face. He rolled his shoulders and breathed deeply, releasing the tension of the interview.

Anita walked past him and paused at the car. 'You didn't mention the affair. Helene and Grant, I mean. She said she had been seeing Grant for months, it seems at the same time as he was seeing June, and his wife.'

'Helene said June didn't know. I don't think it's important.'

'But if June knew, then Eloise may have too.'

'Neither have ever suggested it. Let's not put words in our witness's mouth shall we?'

'Helene said that she felt uncomfortable coming forward about the car because of the affair and her previous friendship with the sisters. All pretty tangled. Grant sure got around...' Anita persisted.

'He did. But that's more a motive for Eloise. The jilted wife.'

'So why not talk to June about it? Gauge her reaction.'

'Because Eloise did it. She was seen in Beesands and returning here. The timeline fits, the evidence fits.'

'And asking June if she knew about Grant and Helene's affair affects this how?'

'Doubt,' Robert said making his way to the curb and the passenger side of the car. 'It casts doubt. Gives June a motive, and makes Eloise into a more sympathetic figure. She's already a nightmare culprit: white, gentle, well mannered. A jury bonding with her as the betrayed wife, that is something we don't need.'

Anita nodded and opened her car door. 'He really was a pig wasn't he? Grant Huxley, I mean. Cheating bastard.' She paused, eyeing Robert.

'His life choices don't matter, Anita. He didn't deserve to die like that. Cheating is bad, sure. But it's not murder. He is the victim in all of this, don't forget that.'

'Sure, but he kinda made his bed, don't you think? I mean, you piss off enough women someone's gonna get ya.' Not waiting for his response, Anita climbed into the car.

Robert frowned, considering her words. Could anything really justify murder? *No*, he thought. But his instant response rang dull. He knew he didn't believe it. If anyone ever hurt Tom... Robert took a deep breath filling his lungs with the sea air, pushing the flood of primal fatherly protection that laced his limbs aside and re-focusing his mind, before following Anita's lead and settling into the car, ready to return to the city.

It was unnerving how thin the line between a good man and a killer could be.

17: Against better judgement

The tequila slid down Harriet's throat. A welcome burn. Around her the dim lights of the Red Lion pulsed to the rhythm of the DJ set, bodies covered in a sheen of sweat despite the outside cold. She grinned at Phoebe. 'God it's good to be out on a Friday!' she shouted across the din. 'No morning alarm to cramp my style.'

Phoebe threw back her head in laugher then leaned over the bar to catch the bar tender's attention. 'Two more slammers,' she yelled. He nodded. In short order another shot slipped down Harriet's thirsty throat. *Fuck, what a week,* she thought. Then shoved it aside. Tonight was not about work. Tonight was about partying.

'So,' Phoebe crooned, dark eyes dancing, 'drunk enough to let me take you home yet?'

Harriet smiled wide and laughed, 'Give me an hour.'

The two friends were jostled by the sea of fellow weekend revellers as they ordered drinks and tried out new pick up lines.

'Against my better interests,' Phoebe drawled, 'Mr wanted-to-go-professional-but-injured-my-knee-so-I-coach-football over there has been eyeing you for ages. Easy pickings, I'd say. And not bad on the eye. Definitely dumb though. But good for the night.'

Harriet swivelled round and took in the fair haired man Phoebe indicated. Slim but broad across the shoulders, shirt a size too small to enhance his physique, his lip curved up at her glance.

'Fuck it,' Harriet said downing the last of her tequila before making her way across the bar to Mr Coach. Behind her Phoebe let out a whoop of encouragement and turned to the group beside her, striking up conversation.

Harriet lowered her lashes and smiled secretly at the man. 'Wanna dance?'

He was nodding to the music, eyes intense. He held up his hand, a wedding ring caught the dim light. 'Gonna be a problem?' he asked.

Harriet smiled darkly, 'Isn't usually,' she said and grabbed him round the waist, hauling him against her body and onto the dance floor.

The music swam around her, sweat licked down her throat, strong arms wrapped around her waist. She pulled him closer, willing his heat into her body, losing herself in the moment, his breath hot on her neck, the touch of his lips on her skin.

Out of nowhere, the details of Danny Flint's rape case slapped her from her subconscious. Images of wild eyes filled with fear flashed through her mind, hands forced above a terrified face, wrists bound, hair bunched in a fist, face forced into the hard dirt, an evil sneer.

'Stop,' she breathed, suddenly desperate for air.

'What?' Laughter in his voice. His hands gripped her hips thrusting their bodies together with the music.

'No,' Harriet said, pressing against his chest, 'Stop!' she shouted.

The man pulled back, stunned. 'Fucking cock-tease!' he shouted, face twisted with the anger of rejected arousal.

'Back off mate!' Somehow Phoebe was there, arm around Harriet, body between her and the furious man. 'Whatever, cunt,' he said dismissively, turning away. Phoebe flipped him off, then gathered a shocked Harriet in her arms and pulled her over to the side of the room.

'You ok?' Phoebe's eyes flashed concern.

Harriet shook her head, taking a deep breath.

'Damn, Harrie,' Phoebe said. 'I thought you wanted to get laid.' She grinned mischievously at Harriet.

'I did. I do. Fuck!' Harriet ran her hands through her hair. 'That was probably my fault... I should apologise.' She went to break away from Phoebe, but her friend held on to her, grip like a vice.

'Woah, there mate,' Phoebe said. 'Firstly, you don't owe that guy shit. No means no, regardless of what was happening before. Got it?' She stared into Harriet's eyes until she saw the understanding she wanted. 'And second, I don't think he wants to talk to you again...' Across the room Mr Coach stood brooding with a group of equally well toned men. Harriet cast her eyes down.

'Hey,' Phoebe said, pressing a finger under Harriet's chin and bringing their eyes level. 'No bad here. You're ok.'

Harriet nodded slowly. 'It's this rape case I'm working. Its just got me all fucked in the head at the moment.' *That and the fact I think Eloise is innocent.*

Phoebe cocked her head to the side, 'Totally understandable. Wanna get out of here?'

'No, I'm fine. I think I just need a drink.'

'White wine coming up,' Phoebe gripped her hand and led her to the bar.

In a matter of moments Harriet was at a table, wine glass in hand, bottle before her, Phoebe talking shit in her ear. She rolled her shoulders, feeling better already. *What a silly turn.* She laughed at herself. So something her mum would say.

Half a bottle later the two friends were laughing and joking like nothing had happened.

Harriet gripped Phoebe's hand. 'Thank you,' she said sincerely.

'Always,' Phoebe said finishing her wine. 'Except right now, coz that one is not getting away.' She pointed at a leggy red head off to the side of the room.

'I thought you invited me home?' Harriet joked grinning widely.

Phoebe shrugged, 'Snooze you loose,' she replied. Then fixed Harriet with serious eyes. 'You ok if I go chat?'

'Of course,' Harriet smiled. 'Go, go.'

'Sure?'

'*Go!*'

Phoebe leaned forward and kissed Harriet's cheek. 'You're still the most beautiful back up plan in my life,' she smirked.

'Fuck off,' Harriet said, pushing her friend away playfully, laughing. Phoebe retreated across the room, hands up in mock supplication. Harriet grinned and poured the rest of the wine into her glass, reaching for her phone. Flicking through her emails she drained the last of the wine and decided it was probably time to head home. She reached for her purse when...

'Fancy meeting you here,' a deep voice said.

Harriet looked up and smiled, 'We have to stop meeting like this,' she returned.

Robert, dressed in a white shirt and jeans, stepped into the bar. And there she was, sitting at a table across the room. Alone. His heart fluttered oddly in his chest and he shook his head. He wasn't yet ready to admit how much he'd been hoping she would be here. He waved to Bobbie to say hi and made his way over to Harriet.

'Fancy meeting you here,' he quipped lightly.

'We have to stop meeting like this,' she smiled. God that smile.

His mind emptied. For a moment he just stood there, frozen. Her eyes flicked to her wine glass, empty. Robert surged into motion, 'Can I buy you a drink?'

'I thought you'd never ask.'

She smiled. Robert headed to the bar.

They chatted for hours. About what, Robert couldn't rightly remember. But the bottle of white he'd bought was empty and the clientele were thinning out. She seemed, different, subdued. Less spicy, but more substantial somehow. Harriet's friend, a tall dark haired woman with eyes of onyx was leaving, hand cradling the butt of a glorious red head. *Lucky lady*, Robert thought ruefully.

'So you got custody?' Harriet was saying. Robert pulled his mind back to the table. They'd been talking about family and Robert had mentioned it was just him and Tom at home. Which wasn't exactly a lie, but... he opened his mouth to correct her assumption but Harriet continued, 'Or you just got him by default coz he didn't want to change schools. Either way, you win. Kept your kid. Odds are well against father's on that score. Good for you.'

Robert smiled and nodded. 'I love my son,' was all he said, for some reason unwilling to properly explain the situation with Gemma and their marriage.

'Of course,' Harriet replied, then checking her mobile, 'It's late. I really should get some sleep tonight.' She grinned at him suggestively then reached for her jacket. 'But I really enjoyed this. Even if it's not really... sensible.'

Robert smiled, 'Just drinks. No shop talk. I think we are good.'

'Yeah,' she replied, 'just drinks.' She hovered before him as if considering, then leaned in and pecked him on the cheek.

'See you in court,' she said, walking away.

'Not if I see you first,' he called.

She spun on a heel and raised a hand in a wave, her sultry lips curved in amusement, then walked out of the pub.

The dark outside was complete as Harriet made her way up the stairs to her apartment, but she didn't mind. She felt light and strangely excited. *Silly woman*, she chided herself, *you're acting like a teenager.* Everything about DS Robert Fields was a warning sign, flashing neon. He was older, divorced or something, a father and working a murder case against her. Not a good set of criteria for starting a relationship, even if it was only casual. And yet... Harriet liked being around him. *I need to smother this*, she thought. Still, the smile stayed on her lips.

She turned the key in her door and crept in quietly, not wanting to wake her brother. She needn't have bothered. The soft glow of the TV illuminated the lounge, the sound of gunfire ricochetting around her living space. Walking into the lounge, Harriet saw her brother stretched over the couch, beer in hand. Next to him sat a shorter man with a wispy beard, beanie snug around his head, hands clasping a Playstation controller. Both men's eyes were firmly fixed on the TV where computer generated characters in army camo ran, ducked and shot their way across the screen. It felt like she'd travelled back in time to her uni days. She scoffed to herself, two grown men wasting their days gaming...

'I don't own a Playstation,' Harriet announced.

Neither man looked up.

'Mine,' her brother answered, monosyllabically.

Ignored, Harriet padded to the kitchen and helped herself to a lager and a packet of crisps before curling up on the floor, back against the couch.

Wordlessly her brother held out his hand for some crisps and Harriet poured a generous handful into his palm. All waited in silence, watching the battle unfold before them. At length Billy's friend tensed and then exclaimed, 'Fucking bullshit!'

'Nah,' Billy countered, 'you just weren't quick enough. Ok, my turn.'

Glumly the friend handed over the remote, eyes registering Harriet.

'Hare, this is Nicky, Nicky, Hare,' Billy offered.

'We've met,' Nicky said.

Harriet cocked her head at him quizzically.

'We were at uni together. I was in your year, but spent most of my time with this dickhead.' He punched Billy in the arm.

'Sorry, I don't remember.'

'No dramas. Big night then hey?' He shamelessly eyed Harriet's stockinged legs. Harriet frowned and reached for her brother's blanket, covering herself up. Nicky's eyes glittered.

Silence fell as Billy started up his campaign and Harriet passed the remainder of the crisps along to Nicky.

'Actually, I knew your client too,' Nicky announced, 'Well, at least her husband. When I did my first degree in 2000.'

Harriet looked up at Nicky sharply, then glared at Billy. 'Bill's not meant to talk about my work,' she said.

'Didn't say nothing Hare,' Billy said, eyes glued to the TV.

'Nah, it's true, he didn't. Saw it on the news. You don't forget Grant Huxley,' Nicky said, eyeing Harriet. 'He was a final year, I was in first. Guess I kinda looked up to him. Real ladies man, always on the pull. Lots of knickers to juggle.' He grinned.

Harriet rolled her eyes. Men and their admiration of each other's conquests. *Lame.* She watched Nicky's unkept face, eyes bright, chin unshaved, wrinkles beginning to frame his eyes. How old was this guy, 35-40? And still talking like a fucking teenager tallying notches on his belt.

'Hot girlfriend too. What was her name... Jinny, Judy, no, June! That's it.'

Harriet's eyes snapped up to Nicky's face. 'You knew June?'

'Well sure, by association.'

'June Lane. Eloise Lane-Huxley's sister?'

'Yeah, pretty twisted hey, marrying your sister's ex. Especially after the pregnancy.'

'What pregnancy?'

'Shhh,' Billy hissed, 'some of us are working.'

Harriet glared at the side of Billy's head, then turned back to Nicky. 'What pregnancy?' she repeated. She didn't lower her volume. *Working, really Billy!*

'June and Grant. Final year. Grant was pissed. They broke up soon after that. Wonder what happened to her. She was fucking hot.'

Gossip spun, Nicky returned his attention to the war game on the screen. 'Watch the bomber!' he exclaimed.

'I know, I know. Shut up.'

Harriet rose, no longer able to stand the staccato of the fake gunfire. Mind whirling she headed to bed.

18: To lose a child

The Devon Expressway slipped past Harriet's window. Brown tree limbs pressed against the invisible barrier of the highway, trimmed mercilessly to maintain traffic safety, about to burst forth in vibrant green foliage with the spring sunshine. But not just yet.

Harriet turned on the air-conditioning and blasted cold air into her face. She wasn't hot. She was tired. Exhausted from the week and drinking with Phoebe (and Robert), Harriet had intended to find her bed and let it keep her until at least midday. But Nicky's announcement about June's possible pregnancy during her uni days had rattled around her head incessantly as she tried to calm her body into sleep. She wasn't sure why yet, but it felt important.

What had happened to that baby? And did its existence matter to her case?

She'd finally accepted defeat at around 8 a.m. and padded to the kitchen for coffee. On the couch, Nicky snored. God knows what time those two had made it to bed. Restless, Harriet had tried to occupy herself reading case files, but fatigue and the niggling sense that she needed to know more about the pregnancy had her checking the time on her phone every few minutes. At 8:23 a.m., she broke and dialled.

'Hello?' the gentle voice of Dorothy Lane answered the phone.

'Hi, Mrs Lane, it's Harriet Bell here. I was hoping to ask you a few questions about your daughter June. Is now a good time?'

'Oh, hello Harriet. Working early! Yes of course, not a problem. What did you want to ask me about?'

'June went to Exeter University in 2000, is that correct?'

'Yes, to study business management and accounting. Came top in her class. We were very proud.'

'And it was during that time that she was dating Grant Huxley?'

113

A short pause and exhale of breath, like a huff. 'Well, yes. Her final year, I think. But as I told you at your office, that is old news. Water under the bridge...'

'Mrs Lane, I need to ask you something quite personal I'm afraid. Please understand I am only trying to connect all the important facts in Eloise's case.'

'Of course, though I don't know what June has to do with it.'

'Mrs Lane, to the best of your knowledge, do you know if June pregnant at the end of her university course?'

Silence. Shuffling. The sound of a door closing. Then, hissed down the line, 'Not here. Can you meet me in Salcombe? At the carpark by the pier. At say 12 noon?'

'Today?'

'Yes.'

'I'll see you there, Mrs Lane.'

So now she drove through the mid morning sunshine as it shone its pale light on the grey roads. Harriet blinked her eyes rapidly to refocus on the grey road that twisted ahead, carrying her to Salcombe. Soon she turned off the highway and onto the narrow paths of South Devon, weaving between hedgerows and stone walls, tiny towns and large farm acreages. The sun breaking through the clouds meant more cars were now on the narrow roads. Harriet had to stop in the eves to let multiple cars and one truck pass as she travelled, but the delay was minimal and soon enough she came to the hilly coastal town of Salcombe. After finding a carpark she strolled to the pier and waited, eyes turned to the sea. The tide was out, leaving the fishing boats resting on their bulbous bellies, anchor chains overgrown with barnacles exposed to the late morning air. A cool sea breeze caught the smell of seaweed sweating in the sun and brought it to Harriet's nose. She could understand why people lived here. Large town, money and opportunity, but too far from the rest of the world for Harriet's taste. Still, it was a beautiful place. *The setting for an idyllic childhood,* she mused. Ellesmere Port it was not.

'Ms Bell?'

Harriet turned and smiled at Dorothy. Dressed in jeans and pumps with a neat woollen jumper wrapped about her to bar the wind from her pale skin, Dorothy looked both smaller and younger than when they met in Harriet's office over three months ago.

'There is a lovely cafe just across the street, the Sea Breeze. Lovely scones. Would that suit?'

'Sounds delicious.'

Harriet followed Dorothy to the Sea Breeze. They ordered scones with Devonshire cream and jam made from the owner's own raspberries. 'I just can't abide store bought stuff,' Dorothy confided. Harriet smiled. Around them fellow patrons read newspapers and sipped tea. It was not yet the season for the Devon coast, but the locals were out in force enjoying the arrival of the warmer weather after the closeted days of winter proper.

Dorothy arranged her hands before her, neatly folded and began,'I'm sorry to drag you down here, Ms Bell.'

'Harriet, please.'

'Harriet,' she paused, 'Mr Lane knows nothing of this particular, trouble. Nor does Eloise. And I hope you can agree it's best it stays that way. Given recent, events.'

She looked down, eyes shadowed. The youth the warm sunlight had revealed on the pier crumpled down into the worries of a much older woman. The mother of a murderer.

Harriet's heart went out to her. 'I am sorry to intrude on such personal matters, Mrs Lane. I wouldn't ask if I didn't think it was important.'

Please don't ask why it is important, she willed silently.

'The workings of the law are not something I understand, Harriet,' Dorothy replied. 'Paul and I are guided by you in all things. We want what is best for Eloise. You must believe that.' She fixed Harriet with wide, tired eyes, full of pain.

'Of course I do,' Harriet rejoined.

Dorothy breathed out a heavy breath of sorrow and resettled herself on the wicker chair.

'In 2000, Junie came home to study for her final exams. It was the first time in four years of study that she did. I didn't think much of it at first. Final year is a greater stress after all. It seemed a natural choice.'

She paused, fingers twisting her gold wedding band and enormous ruby engagement stone.

'It was about a week after she came home that I heard her vomiting. I thought nothing of it, she often went out drinking with friends. While I disapproved of such behaviour so close to her exams, I'd learnt long ago not to try and offer counsel to my June.

'But then I heard her again the next morning, and then later that afternoon and my mind got to putting things together.

'I confronted her over tea and scones,' Dorothy blushed shyly. 'It seems to be my go to in times of challenge.'

As if on queue their waitress, Annabelle, arrived with their order. Despite her avid curiosity Harriet could not help the instant salivation of her mouth and grumble of her stomach as the scent of fresh scones and sweet jam hit her nose. She cut into her scone and lathered on the jam, topped it with lashings of rich golden cream.

Dorothy smiled knowingly. 'Nothing like Devonshire cream,' she said.

Harriet, mouth full of scone and cream, nodded and wiped her lips with a napkin.

'So,' Dorothy continued, 'I asked, and unexpectedly, June didn't resist me.' She paused, eyes far away in the thrall of the recollection of old pain.

Harriet pushed down a stab of guilt. Making her talk of this moment from so long ago, when right now her young daughter faced an even worse fate, it wasn't fair. But then again, nor was life.

'She burst into tears and told me the truth. She was pregnant; Grant didn't want it.' She breathed deeply, 'I held her, told her all the usual platitudes: it's ok, you will get through it, we will work something out, etc etc... we decided to keep it to ourselves until after exams and then we would work out the best way forward, to care for the child.'

'But she never had the baby? Did she?'

'No,' Dorothy said shortly, reaching for a second scone and taking her time over its preparation. Harriet waited, she was experienced enough to let people take their time over their confessions.

'She returned to Exeter for her exams and then stayed there for the summer. We heard little from her. I began to worry. From what I could tell she would have been close to five months along and I wanted her home where I could be a support. Just when I was on the verge of telling Paul everything and demanding we drive to Exeter and collect her, she arrived home.'

Dorothy sipped her tea, watching Harriet over her cup.

Harriet realised, shocked, 'She wasn't pregnant anymore, was she?'

Dorothy shook her head.

'What happened? Did she lose it? I hear miscarriage is much more common than people think... Or did she...?'

'I don't know. I tried to talk to her, but she was back to my old Junie; holding everything close, not sharing. The only thing I know is that she and Grant had broken up.'

'Do you know why?'

'He left her for one of her friends.'

Harriet couldn't help the hiss that escaped her lips. She looked up at Dorothy, shame faced.

'I quite agree,' Dorothy said, her eyes glittering angrily.

'Where was Eloise during all of this?'

Dorothy exhaled a heavy sigh, looking down at her scone she replied, 'Hollydale. Her delusions had increased significantly the Christmas before. June brought Grant down for the holiday. It triggered something in Eloise. She said June threatened to kill her if she went near her boyfriend, which was just preposterous! She started having dreams of blood, visions of June standing over her while she slept. It was out of control. We had to do something...'

She looked up at Harriet, eyes wide in an open plea for understanding. The shame of having committed her youngest child still fresh all these years later. Harriet tried for a reassuring smile, though she felt quite sure it didn't reach her eyes. Eloise had suffered at Hollydale, and as a result had avoided getting help after Jacob's birth caused a resurgence in her symptoms. Had she really needed to be committed? Or just understood?

Dorothy shrugged, 'But, as I said, that was all in the past. Eloise knew nothing about June's pregnancy. And I really don't think Grant rushing off with Helene is anything to do with...'

'Helene?'

Dorothy paused, 'Yes,' she relented, 'Helene was the friend Grant left June for.'

'Not Helene Swift?'

'Well yes, or at least she was Swift then. I don't know about now. How do you know Helene?'

'June borrowed her car on the night of the murder.'

'Oh, I didn't realise they were still in contact.'

Harriet's mind was whirring, 'Dorothy, would you know where Helene lives?'

'You'd have to ask June. Somewhere in Salcombe is all I know. But she works at the Salcombe Health Club. I see her there when I do my Wednesday Pilates. But we don't talk.'

Harriet sipped her tea and let that information filter through her.

A decision cemented itself in her mind.

'Could you point me in the direction of the health club?'

19: The other woman

Harriet stepped through the automatic doors of the Salcombe Health Club. The warmth of the heating system washed over her like a fake summer breeze as she broke through from the scent of the salty coast and into the brine of sweaty gym mats. A tall muscled man glistening from a workout sauntered past her, making no attempt to hide his open appraisal of her black jeans and open neck shirt.

Harriet looked away and rolled her eyes. *No wonder I never stick to my memberships*, she thought. Spying the welcome desk (helpfully labelled, WELCOME in large blue lettering) she wandered over to the reception staff. She picked a young girl, no more than 18 in blonde Heidi plats.

'Hi, I am looking for Helene Swift? I believe she teaches yoga here.'

'You have an appointment love?'

'No, but I was hoping she might be free?'

The girl, tapped at the computer before her. 'She's actually on break. I'll just call up and see if she is free. Who shall I say is asking?'

Harriet paused a moment. *Fuck it.*

'June, June Lane.'

Five minutes later, a slender bronzed woman strolled into the reception. Eyes scanning. Confusion flashed across her face and she turned to the desk. Harriet sprang into action, intercepting her before she could ask a question and give Harriet away.

'Helene Swift?' she asked, proffering her hand to shake. 'Harriet Bell, I am Eloise Lane-Huxley's defence attorney. Could we talk?'

Helene's dark eyes scanned her face, the subterfuge slowly dawning. 'I have a class at one…'

'This won't take long.'

Helene paused, staring at Harriet. For a moment Harriet thought she would simply walk away. She'd only come out to see June... Not Eloise's defence lawyer.

'Fine, this way.'

Harriet breathed a sigh of relief.

Helene led Harriet across the reception and into a small side room furnished with a simple IKEA style table and four plastic chairs. Helene took a seat on one side and looked up at Harriet expectedly. *No warm PT welcome here*, Harriet thought.

She took a seat herself and began, 'I'm sorry to just turn up...'

'It's ok, but like I said, I don't have long.'

'Right,' Harriet paused. 'You have spoken to the prosecution in Eloise Lane-Huxley's case?'

'I have. They asked about a white car. It was the right thing to do.'

'Of course,' Harriet hastened on, 'but I am more interested in before now. Back when you were at Exeter University...'

Realisation dawned on Helene's face and her eyes narrowed, 'You mean about Grant and me? It was a long time ago.'

'Did you know June was pregnant when you got together with Grant?'

Helene glared at Harriet. If looks could kill.

'No,' she said shortly, 'not until later.'

'Do you know what happened to the child?'

'There was no child,' she said. Pausing, she leaned back, crossing her arms across her chest in a strongly defensive gesture. Harriet waited, watching the emotions cycle across Helene's face: anger, refusal, consideration and finally, resignation. 'I didn't know, like I said. But after Grant and I broke up... June came to see me. Told me what went on. He talked her into an abortion. Said they had 'the rest of our lives' for children, just not now. So she got rid of it. We started dating the week after.'

Harriet sat still, stunned and hoped that her face remained neutral.

Recovering she asked, 'That's quite a history. How did you continue your friendship?'

Helene snorted, 'Friendship? Hardly.'

'But you leant her your car?'

Helene sighed, 'I saw Eloise from time to time, at mutual friends parties. Up in London a time or two. But June, no. Time doesn't heal everything. I was surprised when she rang. But I wanted to help.'

Harriet nodded, *Guilt*, she decided, *we all do stupid shit for guilt.*

'You chatted a while and then she took the car?'

'Is that what she said? No, she came in, took the car and left. Couldn't wait to get away from me.'

Harriet cocked her head in question and waited.

Helene eyed her. 'She was in a state, ok? Worked up. I don't know… said, "he's doing it again, I need to get back". I didn't want to give her the car. But after what I did… what could I do?'

'"He's doing it again." Meaning Grant?'

'Who else? The man's a snake. I don't think he's ever kept to one woman for long.'

'Doing what exactly?'

Helene shrugged.

'Who was June worried for?'

Helene looked at her incredulously, 'Eloise! Who else? June has always fought for her sister. I don't know if they told you, but Eloise was hard to come by. Poor Mrs Dot suffered many miscarriages between the two girls, that's why there's so many years between them. Then Eloise was early, sickly. She needed constant care. Care they probably needed to reign in at some point.'

'Meaning?'

She paused, sighed, 'They were controlling, I think. June was free to grow and explore, Eloise was kept locked up safe. It was half the reason she married Grant if you ask me. The man may be a shit, but he'll let you live your own life. And Eloise was so happy in London. I was surprised they convinced her to come back here…'

Harriet paused, frowned. Eloise had implied the exact opposite of Grant's behaviour towards her, that she had to follow his lead or else… *Or else what?* She still didn't know.

'Did Grant treat you, well?'

Derision, raw and direct smothered Helene's face. 'Yes,' she said, sarcasm dripping from her voice, 'He was an angel.'

Harriet's brows drew down.

Helene sighed, 'He was fine,' she said. 'We fucked, that was all. He didn't owe me anything. Just rang when he was in town and we met up. But no, he was never anything inappropriate with me. Unless you count the fact he was cheating of course.'

'Eloise speaks fondly of Torcross, and I've seen no hint of malice in her over the decision,' Harriet said, picking up the other part of Helene's statement that didn't ring true to what she knew of her client.

Helene rolled her shoulders, leaning forward, 'Yeah, well, what would I know? Look, there's nothing else I can tell you about what happened, ok? June called me. She was nervous, worried. She wanted to get back to Eloise, so I lent her my car. That's it, all right?'

'All right,' Harriet agreed quickly.

Helene sat before her, visibly agitated. 'You say Eloise was happy down here?' she said.

'Such has been my impression, yes.'

Helene frowned. 'When I heard they'd split and she'd come back south I was happy for her. Getting away from Grant, I mean. I thought… I thought it would be better for her here, even if she didn't know it,' she huffed a breath. 'Just like her parents, hey? Thinking I know what's best for her.' She shook her head. 'Was pretty wrong about that wasn't I? We all were.'

Harriet stared at Helene in surprise. Then, collecting herself, 'Thank you for your time. It's been very helpful.'

Helene eyed her a moment. 'Look after her,' she said, 'Eloise. She was always such a little, quiet thing… what they say she did. Well, anyway, I have to go.'

'Again, thank you,' Harriet said and left the club.

The shadows stretched long and dull across the grey expressway, the setting sun cutting through the foliage in uneven bursts, shocking her eyes. Harriet barely noticed. Churning through her mind the words of Dorothy and Helene danced around each other, circling, clashing, converging. A pregnancy, the loss of a child and her partner, such a lot for any woman to go through, let alone one as young as June had been. Grant, it seemed, had never taken commitment seriously. And June was clearly jealous of him. Eloise said herself that June warned her away from him. At 13 what threat could she possibly have been?

It did pose the question - was Eloise's claim that June threatened her really a delusion? Or was that just a truth their parents couldn't countenance: that their healthy, ambitious daughter was mistreating their fragile child? It broke the story the Lanes had built around their children. June the brave and strong protector, Eloise the vulnerable child they had to keep close and safe. Had she suffered through the experience of Hollydale for telling the truth?

Helene had observed their over protective treatment of Eloise, called them controlling. Was it more than that? They made no secret of their dislike of Grant and his treatment of Eloise and June. They were also concerned that Eloise would lose the support money if Grant got sole custody of Jacob. Did they somehow arrange for Grant's death in a misguided attempt to protect their daughter and secure the money? Allow the blame to fall on Eloise and see her locked away, safe and sound, forever?

But Eloise was stronger than she appeared. Quiet and shy yes, yet there was an inner strength there that Harriet could not help but admire. She stood accused of the most horrid possibility, that in a forgotten rage she had killed her husband. Yet she stood tall and faced the memory with conviction and strength. How many people could honestly say they would do the same in her position?

Harriet shook her head, there was much to consider, she needed to let her subconscious do some overtime, to fit the pieces together, somehow.

One thing was sure, however. June Lane had a motive.

20: Too far forward

'June is lying. I brought vodka.' Harriet stood in the frame of his front door, black skinny jeans outlining her shapely legs, jacket tight against her shapely curves and the evening chill. Robert looked her over. Eyes clear, a small determined smile on her lips.

'Going to invite me in?' she grinned provocatively, waving the bottle of Absolut before her like a pass card.

Robert hesitated, just a moment, then stepped back opening the doorway for her to pass.

What am I doing? he wondered furiously to himself, pulse racing. At least Tom wasn't home, he was off spending Saturday night with James, again. *Some company would be nice,* he told himself. Unsuccessfully.

Harriet sauntered through his door, head held high, all the spice was back. She wandered across his lounge and into his kitchen, paused a moment scanning the cupboards then took a punt.

Guessing correctly, she pulled down two tumblers and promptly poured out two generous shots of vodka. Robert brushed past her on the way to the freezer, skin tingling at the unexpected contact and pulled out an ice cube tray. He furnished their drinks with ice and Harriet held her glass before her. Watching him over the rim of the glass her eyes danced with a strange intensity. 'Cheers,' she breathed softly over the glass. Plump lips cupped the glass softly before she threw back her head and downed the shot in one. Ice clinking against the glass she poured herself another and made her way into the lounge.

Taking a sip of his own vodka, Robert followed.

In the lounge Harriet kicked off her heels and flopped down onto his sofa, curling her feet up beneath her and leaning back, eyes

123

following him as he entered the room. Where to sit? Harriet's curled legs left space on the sofa beside her, but there was also the one seater on the other side. Robert hovered, caught in a moment of indecision, unsure of how to navigate this strange turn of events.

Harriet's eyes gleamed, a wicked smile curving her lips as she leaned over and patted the sofa beside her, eyebrow raised in challenge. *No choice then*, Robert decided and took a seat beside her, subconsciously resting one leg over the cushions to turn his body towards her but also create a physical buffer between them.

They watched each other, sipping their drinks. The silence stretched. Then Harriet spoke.

'Your boy is out?'

'Sleep over.'

'So just you and me then?'

'Yes.'

Harriet nodded, taking a sip of her drink. 'I went to Salcombe today.'

Robert felt his eyebrows rise. So this was about the case.

'Harriet, we really shouldn't talk about…'

'Did you know June was pregnant with Grant's baby? Not now,' she waved her free hand in dismissal of the notion, 'back in their uni days, when they dated.'

Robert fell silent. Interesting…

'He convinced her to get rid of it. Then he dumped her,' she leaned forward vodka glass swaying before her, 'guess who for?'

She grinned salaciously and leaned back, tossing off the last of her drink and reaching to refill her glass. She held up the bottle in offer to Robert, he nodded, holding out his glass between them. She poured another dollop of vodka into it and settled back.

'Helene Swifter,' she announced.

Well, Robert thought, *that is surprising.*

'Friendship can overcome a lot,' he tried.

Harriet snorted. 'You have a high opinion of friendship.'

She stretched a leg out before her, bringing her foot almost to his knee. Robert forced himself to stillness, fighting the urge to squirm.

'I visited Helene today.'

'Of course you did.'

'She said June was in a state the night of Grant's murder, worried about Eloise. Said, "he's doing it again." What to you suppose she meant by that?'

124

Robert shrugged, 'Eloise wasn't stable, Harriet. And she knew about Grant's plans for Jacob. She probably just wanted to support her sister.'

'But Eloise didn't know about the custody plans, not until you showed her the letter.'

'So she says. June says otherwise. As she told you, she found the letter open after returning home.'

'Can you be responsible for actions and motivations you don't remember?'

Harriet paused, sipping slowly. Her initial drinking fervour seemed to have slowed. Robert didn't know if he was glad of it, or slightly disappointed. He shook his head. *Be glad, you arsehole. You don't want her drunk,* he thought. Or did he? He swallowed down a surge of male guilt mixed with desire and focused on the conversation before him.

'It doesn't matter anyway,' he said doggedly. 'June was in Salcombe when Grant was killed, or driving back to Torcross. This is just conjecture.'

'June *says* she was driving home when Grant was killed. But a white car was seen in Beesands. She had time.'

'Harriet,' Robert said firmly, 'Eloise was seen in Beesands, and returning home. No one saw June. And her alibi does check out. All you're doing is...'

'Creating doubt?' her mouth quirked into an evil grin.

'Harriet...'

'You're right,' she announced, shifting her weight against the couch. 'We shouldn't talk about the case. It's unprofessional.'

Suddenly she was on her feet. Robert knew a moment of disappointment. Leaving already. He wanted her to stay. He wanted to talk, to be with her.

Harriet looked down at him. 'So, are you going to cook us something for dinner or shall we order in?'

Robert stared at her, brain caught a moment in surprise. Then he smiled. 'Do you like Bolognese?'

Robert cooked, Harriet drank, sitting on his kitchen bench for all the world as though it were her own.

They ate in the lounge, drank more vodka. At some point Robert put on a record, Marvin Gaye. Harriet snorted at the choice, then leaned back on his sofa, hands moving through the air before her as she conducted the orchestra in her mind.

They talked. About Brexit, Harriet darkly angry, Robert dutifully understanding; about the pressures of work, Harriet like a terrier on the hunt, Robert longing for more weekends off; about childhood, Harriet briefly, Robert at length, remembering days of easy sun and timeless afternoons playing football. And they laughed, their bodies melting into the sofa, the distance between them, both physical and emotional closing rapidly.

Then Harriet, mastering herself after a fit of laugher leaned forward and placed a hand on Robert's arm. The touch was light, momentary. The touch changed everything,

Their gaze met. A new light dancing in the night dark pools of her eyes. Robert leaned forward. Harriet did too. His eyes dipped to her mouth. It quirked into a smile. He lifted a hand, pushed a lock of her hair back behind her ear and…

The front door banged shut. Robert looked up sharply, then shot to his feet. Harriet turned more slowly. There, in the doorway to the lounge, stood Gemma. Clad in a day suit, short blonde hair fashionably mussed, eyes surprised. She dropped her keys into the bowl on the side table and placed her suitcase at her feet.

'Sorry to interrupt,' she said, voice acidic.

'Gemma, I wasn't expecting you this weekend,' Robert stammered, running a hand through his hair.

Harriet's eyes flicked between them. Then she stood. Surprisingly steady given the half-empty vodka bottle at her feet.

'Is that the time?' she said, not even pretending to check a clock. 'I've overstayed.'

She looked to Robert, 'Good to talk about the case. We need to be sure of all the facts.'

Bending she collected up her jacket and slipped on her heels, nodded to Gemma and made for the door.

'I'll see you out,' Robert said.

'No need,' she brushed passed Gemma, walking fast.

Robert glared at Gemma, who shrugged and went for the kitchen.

By the time he caught up to Harriet she was in the drive, shuffling past Gemma's Honda.

'Harriet, wait, it's not what it looks like…' He reached for her arm, catching her sleeve.

Harriet whirled around, flinging her arm out of his grasp. 'Don't *touch* me,' she hissed, venomously.

'Harriet,' he tried again.

She held up her free hand, 'I don't want to hear it.'

She turned, striding determinedly away.

'At least let me call you a cab?'

'I can take care of myself, thank you very much,' she said, not looking back.

'Harriet, please.'

She rounded on him, stopping so suddenly he nearly bowled into her. He halted, so close he was almost brushing her skin, her lips. His heart was still pounding.

'Harriet...'

'You just be sure,' she said.

Robert felt his forehead crease in confusion.

'Just be sure you have the right sister. Because if you don't, I will tear your case and your *career* apart.'

She spun on her heel and began to walk away.

'Harrie, please,' he called.

'Just be fucking sure,' she called as she hit the street, storming away into the dim light of the street lamps.

'Fuck,' Robert breathed, watching her go. His breathing calmed. Mind pounding with frustration he turned back inside to face his wife.

Robert found Gemma at the dining table, a bowl of cold pasta before her. She'd even helped herself to a vodka. A fresh glass sat at the place opposite her, waiting for him. He slumped into the chair and took up the glass. Taking a large sip, he fixed Gemma with his eyes, 'I wasn't expecting you.'

Gemma shrugged, 'It's my house too. Last I checked.'

'We had an arrangement. Once a month.'

'Next weekend doesn't suit. This one does.'

'That's not fair Gemma.'

Gemma paused, twirling some pasta around her fork and taking a large bite. She chewed slowly.

'Ok,' she conceded, 'my bad. But this situation isn't entirely my fault. I can't help it if you haven't explained your marriage to that young thing.' Her eyes flicked towards the door, contempt splashed across her face. 'What is she? Twenty-five? I mean, really Robert.'

'She is older than she looks.'

'Sure.'

'And it's none of your business, Gemma. What I do with my life and my time is no longer your concern. You left.'

Gemma sipped her drink, took a large breath.

Robert continued before she could speak, 'Look, I don't want this...

tension between us. It's not fair on Tom. That's why I agreed to the visits. For our son. But Gemma, it's been almost a year. I have the right to move forward. You have.'

'All right. I'll call next time. I promise. And, I'm sorry for tonight. You're right, it's none of my business.'

She downed the last of her drink and stood up, stretching her neck. Then walked towards the door, heading for the stairs and the guest room made up for her visits. She paused at the door and looked back at Robert.

'Give her the night to calm down,' she said. 'Ring and explain in the morning. It will be ok. She will understand. If she really likes you, she will understand. I would have.'

She smiled sadly and left Robert in silence, only the bottle of vodka and his own frustrated thoughts for company.

He liked Harriet, really liked her in fact. The situation with Gemma, their separation, pending divorce not yet finalised, he should have told her. But he hadn't wanted to complicate things. And perhaps, somewhere deep down inside, he still wasn't ready to admit he had failed at marriage, as a husband; useless, self indulgent thinking. Gemma was gone. Had been for much longer than the 12 months since she walked out, if he was honest. He needed to move on. *Had* been moving on. And now…

'Fuck,' he breathed and poured himself another glass of the clear, swirling liquid.

21: Not guilty by reason of insanity

The arm chair was soft and comforting, Harriet should have felt relaxed. But she didn't. Across from her Randell Dawes QC was skimming through her latest files, stopping occasionally to ask her a question, or direct her towards more research and detail. So far he seemed mostly pleased with her work. But his scrutiny was not why Harriet felt keyed up, anxious.

She was in Randell's London office in London Square Chambers, the room less dark and forbidding now in early April. She watched Dawes' small shoulders hunched over his desk, wrinkled hands elegantly turning the pages, his face an impassive, unreadable mask. She waited.

At length he leaned back, removing his spectacles and appraised Harriet from his side of the wide oak desk. 'Impressive research and background, Harriet. Your detail from witnesses and the Psychologist are exceptional. There really is little doubt in my mind that the jury is likely to find Lane-Huxley Not Guilty by Reason of Insanity. A short trial, I think.'

Harriet nodded, her own shoulders slumped. She should feel triumphant. Randell Dawes QC had praised her. What a step forward his good opinion would be for her career. And the case looked water tight, solid. A short trial. It was good news. Except...

'What aren't you telling me, Harriet?' Dawes's rich, warm voice filled the space between them. 'Has Eloise said more to cause question over Grant's treatment of her?'

'No, nothing more than that one reference back in February. She won't be drawn further, and no one else seems to think anything untoward was going on.'

His eyes, two small dots in his greying skin, narrowed as he searched her face. 'But there's something.'

He said no more, waiting patiently as Harriet gathered together her thoughts.

She had been practicing this speech all week and throughout the train ride to London. She wanted to present her ideas clearly, dispassionately, as though in Court. To bring Randell with her, like she would a jury, to see her truth; her doubt.

Taking a breath she began, and instantly failed at her plan. 'I... Well,' she sighed, 'Eloise didn't do it, sir. I am more sure than ever. After we last spoke, I viewed everything and when I look at the evidence it's just obvious to me. But, no one else seems to see it.' She looked across at Randell and felt the heat rise in her face. Embarrassed at her messy introduction she opened her mouth to rush on. Randell held up a small hand and gazed at her calmly. Harriet paused.

'Take a moment,' he said. 'Compose your thoughts. Then start at the beginning.'

His old eyes were kind. No hint of scorn or impatience. Harriet smiled, grateful and sat in silence, re-setting her jumbled thoughts. Saturday night with Robert had not helped. The swirl of emotions their time together had ignited, coupled with the utter disappointment of discovering his deceit did not make for calm and logical brainwaves. Harriet pushed aside the memory of the shock and burning shame she had felt when his wife walked in, and focused on this moment. Robert was unimportant. What really mattered was Eloise Lane-Huxley.

'As you know from when we first met, I had some concerns over Eloise's guilt. Back then it was an instinct, a feeling. But now...I just don't believe Eloise committed this murder. And I think I have reasonable doubt.'

Dawes settled himself back in his large chair, hands steepled before him. 'Continue,' he said.

Harriet swallowed. 'We know that Eloise has been unwell. That she has suffered from anxiety her whole life, and from post-natal depression this year. So her loss of memory seems explained. And the facts set out by the DPP suggest she is guilty. She was seen in Beesands and returning to Torcross. She was facing the loss of her son, betrayal by her husband. She was of unsound mind. She went into a dissociative fugue, a rage and taking up her crafting scissors, she walked to Beesands and murdered her husband, then returned home.'

Pausing, Harriet grimaced. 'I concede, it is a strong case,' she sighed.

'However,' Dawes prompted gently.

Rolling her shoulders Harriet leaned forward, 'However, there is also the evidence that points to June.' She took another moment, mind collating. 'She says she was in Salcombe to drop off her car, and the garage confirmed this. But then her story shifts. First she said she caught the bus. Then the witness Helene Swifter came forward to say June borrowed her car, her white car.'

'Explained by June as an error owing to her frenzy after finding her sister covered in blood. A reasonable explanation, surely.'

Harriet frowned, 'Yes, and I know there are many white cars in Britain. And even that she was Grant's girlfriend 20 years ago seems irrelevant due to time. But,' Harriet stood up, began to pace the room.

'There is strong evidence that June was having an affair with Grant during the time leading up to his death. Eloise expected Grant on Fridays. But the hotel records show he was there every Thursday. And the hotel confirms that June visited with him every Thursday. That they shared a meal in his room or in the hotel restaurant each week. Not the most subtle affair to be sure. All while Eloise thought June was visiting their parents in Salcombe. And then there is the baby.'

'You mean Jacob?'

Harriet shook her head, 'No, June's baby. A mutual friend of the sisters told me that June was pregnant with Grant's baby back when they were at university. Dorothy Lane confirmed it. Said June lost the baby and then Grant left her for Helene, the owner of the white car June borrowed and forgot.'

Confusion flashed briefly over Dawes's face. He reached for her notes, bringing his glasses back over his eyes, 'I don't recall...'

'It's not in there yet, sir. I only uncovered this information on the weekend just gone. I tried to write it all down, to structure it. But, I think I needed to talk it out with someone first... to find my thoughts.'

Dawes nodded, waiting.

Harriet forged ahead, 'Helene said that Grant convinced June to have an abortion on the basis that it was too soon to have a child, and they could do so later, once their careers were established. She complied. Told no one. Not even her mother, Dorothy was left wondering what had happened to end the pregnancy. June refused to say. Then Grant left her for Helene.'

Harriet brought her hands together before her, clasping them tight. 'After that history, June and Helene were not friends. Though she originally said she took the bus, June later admitted that she borrowed Helene's car. When she collected the car, Helene said June was in a state, said Grant was 'doing it again.' I think… I think…'

Dawes had sat up straight, eyes fixed on Harriet's pacing body.

'June lost her baby because of Grant. He betrayed her. Now, 20 years later June remains single and without a child of her own. She finds herself living with her nephew, who she comes to love like a son. She falls into having an affair with Grant. She is a mix of emotions - guilt over her betrayal of her sister, but also the joy of having a child *and* the man she has always loved. Then the letter comes. Grant is going for sole custody, based on Eloise's mental state…'

Harriet stopped and looked at Dawes, 'She had her baby again. She had Jacob. A replacement for the child she lost twenty years ago. And Grant was going to take that away from her. He was 'doing it again', taking a child. So she killed him.'

Randell cocked his head to the side. 'Using her sister's scissors?'

'The perfect cover is it not? Use Eloise's scissors. Drop your car to a garage in Salcombe. Say you caught a bus, but really take the car of someone you used to know. Someone who owes you. Drive to Beesands. Stab Grant. Go home and clean up. If you make it back in time no one will know.'

'Except your sister, who is at home.'

'Your sister who told you she would be out walking with Jacob and the dog, but it rained, so she was home early. June even said how she'd forgotten her jacket when she went to Salcombe, not expecting the weather…'

'So Eloise was unexpectedly home. June returns covered in blood. Eloise goes into shock and can't remember any of what happened.'

'Only that her sister was covered in blood. And that she couldn't find her scissors. She couldn't find them because June took them. They were never in the house for Eloise to find!'

Harriet slumped down into her chair, suddenly exhausted and rested her hands on her knees. She looked up at Randell and waited, pensive.

Dawes's eyes were far away, shifting side to side, calculating. Harriet forced herself to breathe, the hope of understanding was almost choking her.

Then Dawe's eyes met hers and the hope dissipated, leaving her more exhausted than ever. She sat back in her chair and waited.

'It is a good theory Harriet. A strong theory,' he began. 'But it has some holes. And if we run the defence that she *did not* do it, we cannot risk holes. That path leads to prison.'

He paused, placing his hands on the desk before him. 'The car discrepancy is interesting, but a dangerous tactic before a jury. Asking June about it gives her leave to discuss her distress at finding her sister covered in blood. We have to assume her emotion would be very believable.

'But that's not the biggest challenge. Eloise was seen in Beesands and returning home in her jacket. June was not. Eloise left her son unaccompanied, indicating she was already distressed before her sister returned home. The DDP's claim that she found the custody application and it triggered her mental illness fits. Additionally, Eloise's jacket and her shirt were covered in blood. June saw the jacket on the couch when she came home, where Eloise had discarded it.'

'June could have lied.'

'It is most common for one to remove one's wet jacket when returning indoors,' Dawes said calmly. 'Expected behaviour sits with June's story. The jacket was bloody before June arrived, which rather undermines your theory.'

Harriet chewed on the inside of her cheek. 'I'm missing something. It's like the key is right there before me, but I just can't get it in the lock.'

Dawes fixed her with his eyes. 'Then walk the case Harriet. Review the evidence. Place all the pieces before you and see what is missing. But if it isn't there, then you have to accept it. We can't make the facts what we want. Most often our clients are guilty, Harriet. That is the nature of defence.'

Harriet nodded, solemn, defeated.

'So, as we are in Court for arraignment in under a week, shall we get back to the case at hand? Not Guilty by Reason of Insanity, Automatism.'

'Of course,' Harriet replied forcing the disappointment and doubt aside, and pulling her chair closer to Randell's desk in preparation.

'Right, these are the details I need more on…'

Hours later Harriet walked through the grey twilight of London, the dirty cream stone buildings channelling the evening breeze down Embankment. She looked out over the Thames, the dark waters reflecting the first lights of the city at night, sparkling pink, purple and blue over the tidal current. The city felt alive with promise, possibility and adventure. Great things were done here. Great and terrible things.

Pulling her coat around her against the spring evening chill, she joined the throng of commuters on the steps into the station. The scent of warm pastry drifted to her nose and she diverted momentarily to grab dinner on the run, a warm pie to enjoy on her journey home from Paddington. Running for her train she pondered the days ahead. Five days to carry out Randell's directions. Five days to finalise the evidence. Five days to come up with a plan to prove that Robert Fields was wrong. The heat of desire scored her cheeks at the thought of his dark eyes. No, he didn't deserve her interest. She'd thought he was different, but he was just another unreliable man like her father, like Grant Huxley, like Tyler fucking Marks. And Harriet wouldn't see Eloise lose her freedom because of another man's arrogance. She had to focus.

Because she was sure, more sure than she had ever been of anything before. Sure that Eloise Lane-Huxley was innocent. It was no longer just about creating doubt. Now it was about justice.

April

22: Arraignment

Harriet had failed.

Eloise sat motionless in the courtroom, her blonde hair pulled back into a long plait, the dark roots of her re-growth sat like a cap over her crown. She glanced Harriet's way, unease in her eyes. Harriet smiled reassuringly and Eloise smiled back, lips trembling.

It was done. Plea entered: Not Guilty by Reason of Insanity, Automatism. The prosecution had not challenged it. Trial start date set for Friday April 5. Beside her Randell was picking up his notes and slipping them neatly into his briefcase. Court officers arrived to return Eloise to The Orchard. Harriet nodded to her and gave a small smile. Eloise, tears in her eyes now, waved back. How much did she understand of what had just happened? Harriet wondered, fighting the distress that pressed on her chest. The heavy weight of failure.

She had returned home last week and worked through the nights, combing through witness statements, DNA, forensics, anything she could find as she sat in her dining room, the background music of Billy's war games filling the silence. Her days were filled with Randell's requests. Between them they finalised the case, and it was solid. Even if Harriet *felt* it was wrong. She couldn't prove it. No, the case for Automatism is strong. The right defence.

Frowning to herself she glanced over at Bella and Don Huxley, Grant's parents. They sat straight backed, faces fighting to hide the storm of emotions that must be raging just below the neutral surface they strained to cultivate. It was the first time Harriet had seen the bereaved in person. The defeat that sat heavily across their countenance sank into her guts. In losing Grant, their only son, they had lost everything. Two rows back from the Huxleys sat the Lanes, up from Salcombe for the day. Dorothy Lane, sitting primly by her husband, watching Eloise being led away. Only June was absent, presumably caring for Jacob; a courtroom was no place for a child. Harriet was glad of it. She wasn't sure how she would react to the sight of the woman whose innocence she so strongly doubted, yet whose guilt she could not prove. Harriet felt her heart stutter. Seeing these people all together in a room: parents all facing the loss of a child, in one way or another, bound by their history and their love of Jacob, what challenges and pain they had to face. Alone and together. A unity and peace destroyed by the murder of Grant Huxley.

Facts were king, and it seemed her instincts had been wrong when it came to Eloise Lane-Huxley.

Sighing to herself she gathered up her notes and followed Randell out of the courtroom.

'Harriet, wait up!' a familiar voice called behind her.

Harriet rolled her eyes, slowing her stride as she continued along the corridor out of the court house. Randell, walking beside her, caught her eye and said, 'I will see you at my office on Wednesday, 2 p.m.?'

'Yes, it's in my diary.'

'All right,' he glanced up at the man now standing waiting at Harriet's back. A small frown creased his aged brow. 'You did well today Harriet,' he said kindly. 'Don't forget that.'

'Thank you,' Harriet managed. 'See you Wednesday.'

Without another word Randell turned and walked away.

Harriet took a deep breath and faced Robert Fields. Sitting on the opposite side of the court that morning had been the first she'd seen of him since *that* Saturday. He'd smiled at her. She'd averted her eyes, quickly. Not the time for those emotions.

'It's good to see you Harriet,' Robert began awkwardly, hope in his eyes.

Harriet huffed an annoyed breath, 'What do you want DS Fields?' she said sharply. 'I have a trial to prepare for. As do you.'

The hope faded from his face, 'Harriet, about Saturday night. It wasn't what you think.'

'No?' Harriet drawled sarcastically. 'So that wasn't your wife unexpectedly returning home for the night?'

'Well…'

'The wife you lead me to believe was no longer in the picture?'

'I…

'Look,' Harriet snapped, her patience at an end. 'I don't know why you're worried. Nothing happened. This,' she gestured between them, 'this was only ever about the case. I came to warn you, nothing more. If you got other ideas that's your problem, not mine.'

'Harriet, please. You know that's not strictly true.'

Harriet's eyes narrowed fiercely, 'Do not presume to tell me what I do and do not know DS Fields.'

'Harriet, please let me explain.'

'Save your breath,' Harriet snapped. 'It's irrelevant anyway.'

'It's not irrelevant…'

'It is. Because I *don't* care. Now, if you'll excuse me. I have a busy afternoon and a client to speak with. Good afternoon DS Fields,' she said and walked briskly away.

Later that evening as Harriet and her brother sat slumped on her couch, neck deep in pizza grease and beer, the buzzer for her apartment sounded loudly across the room.

Harriet looked over at Billy in surprise, 'You ordered something else?'

'Nup,' Billy shrugged, eyes not leaving the TV. Grand designs, the big reveal. It was a repeat, Harriet had seen it before. But she enjoyed the scenes at the end of this one, when you got to see just how badly the build had gone and how compromised the final result was. Sighing, she heaved herself up out of the couch and padded to the buzzer.

After exchanging a few words down the wire she stepped back, shocked.

'So, who is it?' Billy called.

'Crystal,' Harriet murmured.

'What!' Billy's voice echoed from the lounge, She heard her brother stalking quickly to the entranceway. A soft knock sounded on her door just as Billy came up beside her.

'Shit,' he breathed, quickly running his hands through his hair and wiping pizza grease from his chin. Harriet looked him over and frowned.

'Go change, freshen up,' she said. 'I'll mind Crystal until you are ready.'

His eyes whipped to hers, 'Sure?'

'Yes, now go!' She shoved him up the hall and turned to the door. Smoothing out her shirt and quickly licking off a drop of red tomato sauce from the corner of her mouth, Harriet opened the door.

And almost lost her breath.

There before her stood the most beautiful woman Harriet had ever seen. Crystal stood a good two inches taller than Harriet, not that that was much of a challenge, but it was her presence, the way she held herself that caught the eye. She stood calm and still, dark skin glowing in the corridor light, hair braided to her head, one hand cupping the swell of her baby. She looked like a fertility goddess. *Carrying my niece or nephew*, Harriet realised, stunned.

She had known about the pregnancy since Christmas of course, but seeing Crystal's belly, curving out from her floral dress and jacket made it suddenly very real.

Crystal smiled at Harriet, genuine warmth in her eyes.

'You must be Harriet,' she said, voice rich with kindness. 'You could never deny Billy was your brother. I'm Crystal.' She smiled again.

Harriet stood mute a moment more, then forced herself into action.

'Yes, I'm Harriet. I'm so pleased to met you Crystal. Please come in.'

Crystal nodded and stepped into the apartment. 'Billy's just freshening up,' Harriet explained, locking the door behind them. 'Come with me. Can I offer you tea? Juice?'

'A water would be lovely,' Crystal replied as they came into the lounge.

'Please, take a seat,' Harriet gestured to the couch, then groaned inwardly and rushed to clear up the pizza boxes and scattered beer bottles. It looked like a bunch of uni students lived here, not a respected solicitor. Shame flushed her cheeks. She certainly couldn't deny being Billy's sister, not living like this.

'Don't fuss,' Crystal said, 'I've arrived unannounced and you are family. You have no need for appearances with us.' She patted her bulging belly and then eased herself down onto the couch. Harriet bustled into the kitchen and filled a glass of water from the tap. *Was tap water ok for unborn babies?* She didn't know. Unsettled she rushed back in to Crystal.

'Ah, thank you!' Crystal sighed, taking the drink and giving Harriet a smile as though she'd presented her with a diamond. She gulped the water down and settled back into the couch. Harriet hovered a moment, unsure if she should take up the free spot on the couch, before pulling over a dining chair and perching in front of Crystal.

Crystal looked up at her. 'I'm sorry. I owe you an explanation. It must seem very rude to you that I have just appeared at your door.'

'No, it's ok, really,' Harriet stammered, mind still bemused by this vision before her. *What on earth does she see in Billy?* she thought.

Crystal nodded, eyes creasing in amusement as though she'd read Harriet's unspoken words. 'I thank you for your understanding. I didn't want to ring, in case Billy chose to be out when I arrived. It's been too long enough since we talked, I think. Time to resolve this silly tiff. There is Esmerelda to consider.'

'Esmerelda?' Harriet eyed Crystal's belly, joy spreading through her chest. 'It's, it's a girl?'

Crystal smiled indulgently and smoothed her shirt over her stomach. 'She is.'

'Esmerelda is a lovely name,' Harriet offered.

'Isn't it?' Crystal agreed enthusiastically. 'Anyway,' she continued, 'I want Billy home. And you want your apartment back too, I am sure.' She scanned the lounge room, the detritus of 6 weeks of Billy clearly on display. A wry smile curving her lips

'It's probably time.' Harriet agreed.

Just then Harriet heard the scuff of Billy's shoes on the floor and looked up. He'd washed his face, changed to a blue shirt Harriet didn't know he owned and was wearing, cologne? She blinked in surprise. Billy shot her a hard look, a warning. Harriet cleared the surprise from her face and stood. 'Well,' she said, 'I've much to do before Friday, so I'll leave you both to it. And Crystal, the spare room is made up fresh. Billy rarely uses it,' she paused, inwardly cursing herself for mentioning her brother's slovenly couch habits. 'You are very welcome to stay the night. I don't imagine you would be driving back to Ellesmere tonight.'

'That is most kind Harriet, thank you.'

'Yeah, cheers, Hare,' Billy echoed as he walked passed her, eyes fixed on Crystal. His face wore an expression of reserved hope and something else… wonder.

'Woah, you got huge,' he exclaimed, taking in Crystal's belly full of baby girl.

Crystal pressed her lips together, the first sign of annoyance Harriet had seen the woman reveal. That didn't bode well.

'But still so beautiful,' Billy finished.

Crystal's eyes glowed with love as she gazed at Billy. Her brother crossed the room and pulled Crystal into his arms. 'I'm sorry my love,' he said into her neck. Crystal didn't reply, but she brought her arms up around him and buried her face in his chest.

Harriet breathed a quiet sigh of relief and exited the room as silently and swiftly as she could, collecting up her notes and heading for the sanctuary of her room and her work.

A soft knock broke into Harriet's subconscious, pulling her from sleep. She blinked against the glare of her ceiling light, still on. She lay sprawled on her bed, surrounded by papers, legal texts and notes. Sitting up she rubbed her tired eyes. Had she dreamed the knock?

'Hare?' Billy's voice whispered through the door. Harriet sighed and came to her feet. She opened the door. There stood Billy, two cups of steaming tea in his hands.

'Crystal's sleeping,' he said, by way of explanation.

Harriet nodded and opened the door wider, letting him in. He took up a spot on one side of her bed, head resting against her fluffed pillows. Harriet flopped down beside him and took the offered mug of tea.

'How'd it go?' she asked.

Billy sipped his tea. 'Going home tomorrow, ' he said.

'Just like that?'

'Just like that.'

Harriet nodded, savouring her tea. Billy had brewed a proper pot, not just an instant tea bag. She often forgot just how nice a proper brew was. Leaning back into her pillows, Harriet enjoyed the silent company of her brother. An odd sense of loneliness poked at her heart. No matter how messy and annoying Billy could be, it had been nice having him here, with her. She'd been alone in this apartment since he left to get clean. Why hadn't she ever moved out? Found somewhere bigger, nicer? Got a roommate?

'We'll visit again soon,' Billy said, as if sensing the shift in her mood. 'And once Esmerelda is born, you'll have to come up more often. She's gotta know her Aunty Hare.'

Harriet smiled and shoved him playfully.

'Why Esmerelda?' she asked.

'Crystal's grandmother. She's the one who came over from Spain. Died last year. Seems right.'

Harriet nodded. 'And...' she paused bracing herself for Billy's usual hostile reaction to questioning, but she had to ask, 'what about work?' she finished.

'Crystal's got a cousin who's starting up a new garage in Wrexham. Said he's happy to take me on. He specialises in older cars, tractors and the like.' Excitement buzzed in Billy's voice as he described the work. And Harriet realised with a start that it was an excitement that had always been there when he talked about machinery, she'd just never heard it before.

'Sounds really good Bill,' she said.

'Yeah,' he agreed.

They fell silent again. Just two siblings alone with their thoughts, sharing space and tea.

Billy broke the silence, 'Thank you Hare, for everything,' he began. 'I think I got scared. Of Esmerelda, of Crystal, of all of it, you know? I needed some time, some space to work through it all. Thanks for letting me stay.'

'You've got a key,' Harriet grinned at her brother, 'anytime.'

Billy huffed a soft laugh and lowered his head to rest on Harriet's shoulder as he had when they were children. Harriet leant her head on his and sighed.

'I'm happy for you Bill,' she said. 'Truly.'

Billy sat up, looking into her eyes.

'I see it,' Harriet continued, 'this job, this life... with Crystal with your baby girl. It looks good on you. I see it.'

Billy's eyes seemed to fill with water. He turned away and coughed. Harriet smiled knowingly to herself. Composed, Billy turned back to her.

'Thanks, Hare,' he said, 'that means everything.'

23: The scene of the crime

The sun was warm, the air cool and crisp. Salt and seaweed. Sun and sand. Harriet stared out at the waves of Beesand's beach and took a moment to just breathe. Her eyes followed the coast, taking in the curve of the land reaching out to Start Point Lighthouse, another hour's walk away. *Would be a beautiful walk,* she mused, *one day.*

She'd driven down over her lunch break, chicken wrap in hand. She'd been unable to focus on her paperwork, Eloise, the trial, fucking Robert Fields had all crowded in, demanding her attention. Frustrated, she had given up, told her secretary she had to see a witness and, wrap in hand, jumped in her car and drove. It would be nice to say she didn't know where she was going until she pulled up at the car park at Torcross beach, but the truth was far less fatalistic.

Harriet couldn't get Torcross and Beesands, Eloise and June, the murder of Grant Huxley and her doubt as to which sister was truly guilty, out of her head. She'd gone over the evidence, time and time again. She knew Randell Dawes was right, the evidence was clear. Her client, gentle sweet, blue eyed Eloise, was a murderer. All be it an unwilling one. Yet, try as she might, she couldn't shake the feeling that they were wrong. That there was something, *something* in the evidence that she had missed. The 'smoking gun' to Eloise's innocence.

So she'd driven to Torcross and walked the coastal path to Beesands, following in the fateful foot steps Eloise took on November 15, down to the sands of Beesands. There she stood, surveying the sea, hair streaming behind her in the breeze, sunlight glinting on the blue currents. 'What have I missed?' she whispered to the waters. Only the gentle waves of a calm spring day replied.

A cluster of clouds drifted over the sun, casting the land in pale shadow. Harriet suppressed a shiver, the sun was warm, but she was still on the coast and the breeze was brisk. Pulling her jacket closer around her she turned and began her walk back up the hill to Torcross.

It was a beautiful walk, really. All green pastures, dazzling blue waters and crisp horizons. Harriet's breath came hard as she topped the hill. She paused gazing back over the vista, catching her breath and taking in the view. *The perfect route for Ramblers,* she thought, imagining the groups of retirees dressed in their bright rain jackets, hiking sticks in hand, strolling the coast, stopping at the various pubs dotted along the way for refreshment and sustenance. She hoped the murder wouldn't impact tourism to the area too much in the coming season.

Ducking under the heavy foliage of the hill top, she began her descent to Torcross beach. It was a steep descent. Dry now in the warmer spring winds, but on the night of Grant's death the path would have been muddy, slick with winter rains and rotting leaves. Treacherous. Yet Eloise, driven mad by the fear of losing her son, had scaled this cliff as the dark clouds of an offshore storm gathered over head. Crafting scissors clutched in her palm. Swift and sure-footed.

A cluster of stones gave beneath her foot and Harriet clutched a low hanging tree branch to steady herself, narrowly missing landing in the dirt and ruining her work trousers. Her gym trainers were not for hiking. Shaking off the shock, she continued down the path to the small group of beachside restaurants and cafes of Torcross proper. The sun was still high overhead, but the clouds had grown thicker, casting more and more of the pebbled beach into shadow. Walk completed and no witness worth visiting (June would not appreciate her dropping in she was sure) Harriet found herself at a loss. She should return to her office in Exeter. Work late, finish her documentation but... she found herself turning into the small pub on the water front and ordering a glass of wine.

A young girl with hazel eyes poured her a generous glass and Harriet made her way outside to sit in the breeze that blew in off the bay. It had been a long winter, and even the gathering shadows couldn't convince her to stay indoors. She took a seat and settled into her own company, sipping her wine and gazing out to the horizon. A few fellow walkers ambled past, throwing her the occasional nod, wave, or 'good day'. One especially fluffy and friendly golden labrador snuffed her hand and gifted it a lick before her owner caught up and pulled the dog away, smiling an apology which Harriet waved off. She loved dogs. In the waters, a lone swimmer, wetsuit glistening in the sun, cut determinedly through the waves. Harriet felt the warmth of the wine coil along her limbs and breathed out the tension of the day. Slowly a heavy acceptance settled into her bones. The trial would go ahead. Eloise would be found Not Guilty by Reason of Insanity and sent to The Orchard indefinitely, and Harriet would go on. On balance, it was the right outcome. Though her heart persisted in its misgivings, the evidence pointed to Eloise, not June. No matter what Harriet wanted to believe. It was time to accept it.

The door to the pub creaked open and the young lady who had served her wine came out bearing a cup of coffee. She smiled at Harriet as she approached and placed the cup down before her.

'Oh,' Harriet said, 'no sorry, I didn't order this.'

'On the house,' the girl smiled again, 'from dad.' She gestured inside with one hand, flicking her fringe out of her eyes with the other.

Harriet nodded slowly, 'Your dad is David then?'

'Yep,' the girl confirmed. 'Said you deserve it. We all know how much you've done for Eloise... She did an awful thing, we know. But she was still a part of us here. We know she needs help.' The girl paused. Harriet smiled, 'Well, thank you for saying that,' she said, chest tight. 'I wish there was more I could do.'

A small frown creased the girl's brow then smoothed quickly, 'Not sure how that could be true,' she said and smiled again, warmly.

Harriet nodded and took a sip of the coffee. Hot and bitter.

'Oh, delicious. You made this?'

The girl grinned, 'I took a barista course in Salcombe over the winter. Glad you approve.'

'Very much. Tell your dad thanks,' Harriet said, as acknowledgement of the free coffee and to indicate the end of their conversation. But the girl didn't move. Just stood before Harriet, eyes scanning her face.

Harriet waited a moment, giving the girl space. She was clearly working up to something.

Finally, she breathed in, 'I was there, you know. That day when Eloise...' She trailed off.

Ah, Harriet thought.

'Would you like to take a seat? I'm sorry, I didn't catch your name.'

'Sara, thanks.'

Sara slipped her lithe frame down onto the bench opposite Harriet and clasped her hands before her. She picked at a fingernail a moment then continued, 'I dropped Masie off. We live together in Kingsbridge. She does art school in Salcombe. She's almost always late back on

Thursdays so I drove her down. Stayed and took Benny for a walk, Benny's my Westie.'

'Lovely dogs Westies, when I was a child a neighbour of mine had one,' Harriet said. Something was clearly troubling the girl, finding common ground was always helpful to calm nerves.

Harriet waited.

'I was down on the beach when I saw her, Eloise, I mean. She was walking along the foreshore, fast.'

'Yes, Mason said she saw her through the window of the hotel,' Harriet said gently, suppressing her annoyance. *I know, I know she was seen there*, she thought, *don't rub it in.*

'She looked, stressed, worked up. I don't know. Not like normal Eloise,' Sara paused. 'I thought of talking to her. She seemed to need something. But I didn't... I was tired and it was cold and Benny had rolled in some seaweed so I knew he'd need a bath. So I just got back in the car and went home.'

She looked up at Harriet, her eyes dark with guilt, hands wringing before her. 'When I heard the news I...' she swallowed. 'Maybe if I'd stopped,' she said. 'Maybe if I'd have taken a moment and said hello. Asked how she was. Maybe then she would have known someone cared, you know? Maybe she wouldn't have... and Grant would still be...'

'Sara, no,' Harriet said, leaning forward and placing her hand over Sara's own, the warmth of her palm seeping into Sara's icy knuckles. 'This isn't on you, love. Eloise was in what is called a 'fugue state'. She wasn't herself. Probably wouldn't have even known it was you if you had talked to her. In fact,' Harriet paused, set her features with serious sincerity and fixed Sara with her eyes, 'in that condition who knows what Eloise may have done if you had interrupted her? It's better that you didn't.'

Sara's eyes scanned Harriet's face, searching for truth. Slowly the tension in her face slackened and she slumped visibly before Harriet. She nodded, small and sad.

Harriet leaned back, 'So,' she said, voice light, 'I guess you are sure it was Eloise? No doubt? Hood didn't conceal her face?' She huffed a laugh and sipped her coffee again.

Sara looked up in confusion, brow furrowed again.

Harriet waved a hand. 'No, no sorry. Bad joke. Just my regret,' she said. *Geez Harriet, get it together*, she chastised herself.

Sara shook her head. 'No, that's not it.' A pause, expression

146

perplexed. 'It's only, well, Eloise wasn't wearing a hood.'

Harriet cocked her head at Sara. 'Well I guess she didn't have it up then, it wasn't raining until later.'

'No, as in she wasn't wearing a jacket with a hood. Only a light cotton dress jacket. I remember thinking how cold she must have been. It really was chilly that night.'

Harriet stared at Sara, her thoughts had slowed, like they were trying to move through molasses. 'Light dress jacket,' Harriet whispered to herself. Something clicked in her memory. 'Sara, can I show you something?' she asked, voice urgent.

'Sure.'

'Just give me one second.'

Harriet scrambled to her feet and raced to her car parked behind the pub. She threw open her car door and pulled out her folder of notes. Flicking through she found the two photographs she wanted and rushed back to the pub. Sara was still sat on the bench, eyes watching the swell of the sea. She smiled as Harriet approached, question in her eyes.

'You remember the jacket Eloise was wearing?'

'Yes, well, I think I do.'

'Was it this one?'

Harriet swivelled a large photo of a dark blue rain jacket, white inner lining stained with deep red blood. Sara grimaced, eyes flicking up to Harriet.

'Sorry,' Harriet said, 'I know it's graphic. But this is important. Is this the jacket you saw Eloise wearing?'

'Well, no. This is clearly a rain jacket. Eloise was in a tight jacket. I remember thinking just how small she was. I was more than a little jealous of Eloise's body...' she frowned, guiltily.

'What about this one?' Harriet pushed a second image before Sara. A dark green cotton dress jacket with three quarter sleeves, golden buttons down the arms. The red of blood less obvious on the dark material, but still visible.

'Yes, that's it!' Sara said, 'It's such a cute cut. Or at least it was. See? Only light. She would definitely have been cold. I was in my winter coat.'

Harriet stared at Sara. 'You are sure?'

'Positive.'

Harriet swallowed and stood up. 'Thanks again for the coffee,' she said gathering up her folder. She turned and began to stride away, then paused and looked back at a surprised Sara.

'It wasn't your fault, Sara. It wasn't.'

Sara nodded. 'Safe drive home.'

'Thanks,' Harriet waved and rushed to her car. It wasn't home time yet.

Back in her Exeter office she scanned through the witness statements hands shaking. 'Come on, come on, come on'!

She stopped dead.

There it was. The mix up. The oversight. She grabbed up her phone and dialled.

'DS Robert Fields.'

'Robert, it's Harriet. Are you in your office?'

'Harriet, hi, I was actually going to call you.'

'Are you in your office or not?' Harriet snapped.

'Yes.'

'Don't leave, I'm coming over.'

Harriet bustled into Robert's office. A quick scan of the desks found his dark hair and handsome face. Her stomach flipped, her mouth dried. Lord but he was attractive. 'Enough,' she hissed to herself and crossed the room, determination in her stride. He looked up and saw her. Smiled. Harriet didn't respond. His smile faded and she saw the dark smudges under his eyes, the fatigue lining his face. Sympathy reached out to him, an ache pulsing in her heart. She slapped it away. He didn't deserve it.

Flopping her notes down before him, Harriet's gaze bored into him. 'The jackets are wrong,' she began.

'Jackets?'

'Eloise's jacket. I just spoke to a witness in Torcross. Eloise wasn't in a rain jacket at Beesands. She was in her dress jacket. The one she was wearing when you brought her in for questioning. She was never in the rain jacket.'

'Harriet, wait, slow down,' Robert held up a hand to placate her.

Harriet stared down at him. So close she could smell his aftershave. Her mind emptied. *Get it together Harriet*! she snapped to herself. A quick shake of her head and she reset.

'Ok, look,' she pulled over a chair from a neighbouring desk and flicked through the photos. 'My witness saw Eloise at Beesands that night too. Saw her in this jacket.' She pointed to the image of the green cotton jacket. 'Not this one,' she indicated the rain jacket.

'So, I checked the witness transcripts. In her first statement Mason said she saw Eloise in a 'dark jacket.' It was only later when she was reinterviewed that it changed to a 'rain jacket'. Which was after the neighbour, Margaret Ives, was interviewed about seeing Eloise in her hood returning home. Read the transcript.'

Robert flicked his eyes up to her, wary. 'Read it!' Harriet insisted.

He scanned the follow-up interview. Closed his eyes and let out a heavy breath.

'You see? PC Stevens didn't ask Mason what Eloise was wearing. He stated it to her. 'So you saw Eloise in a dark rain jacket?' and Mason agreed. He put the rain jacket into her statement. Not intentionally, probably. But it wasn't what she originally saw. Which means it wasn't Eloise that Margaret Ives saw retuning home in a rain jacket at 6:30 p.m. on the 15th of November. It was June. June in a rain jacket that was covered in blood. June lied.'

Robert looked up. Their eyes met. Hers alight with discovery, his dull with resignation.

He shook his head.

Harriet sat back. 'What?' she demanded.

'Like I said, I was going to call you...'

'Look, I don't care. Things between us aren't important right now. Robert, focus...'

'Harriet,' he said, voice firm.

Harriet stopped.

'Not about... us. I was going to call you about the case. There's been a development.'

'A development?'

Robert ran a hand through his hair, sighed. 'We've just arrested June Lane.'

24: June Lane

June Lane sat across the table, blue eyes wide, hands neatly folded in her lap. Robert watched her face as Anita performed the interview formalities. June's legal aid lawyer, a Mr Adam Peters, looked on with barely concealed disinterest. She looked up at Robert, eyes full of questions. Robert rolled his shoulders, worked to keep his face neutral and calm, to hide the turmoil of emotion that raged within him.

'Ms Lane, some new evidence has come to hand that we would like to speak to you about,' Anita switched from introduction to investigation mode smoothly. Robert sat up.

'What can you tell me about this?' Anita asked.

'For the tape, DI Shan is showing Ms Lane exhibit 37A. A photo of a fishing knife found at Torcross Lake,' Robert chimed in, voice hoarse.

Anita slid the knife photograph across the table to June.

She started shaking. Her eyes flicked up scanning between Anita and Robert.

'No comment,' she whispered.

Robert frowned. That wasn't good. She always talked.

'Take a closer look, Ms Lane,' Anita said firmly, her eyebrows drawn down in a frown.

June's head was shaking. 'No comment,' she repeated. Mr Peters sat forward, suddenly engaged in proceedings.

'Shall we tell you what we know then?' Anita continued, conversational. 'All right. This fishing knife was turned into Kingsbridge Station two days ago. It was found by the lake at Torcross, the one just across from the beach.'

'Near your house,' Robert added. June glanced at him, betrayal in her eyes. Robert fought down the shame that surged in his chest at that look. *Why do I feel guilty?* He wondered. *I didn't lie.*

He fought for focus.

'Some teenagers were rowing on the lake late last year,' Anita went on. 'One threw the other's shoe into the brush on the lake shore. Having a lark. You know teenagers.' Anita scrunched her nose as if enjoying the thought of cheeky youth. Youth only a few years younger than herself in truth. Robert shifted his weight.

'The boy who lost his shoe went searching in the brush to find it. Can you guess what he found instead? This knife.' Anita tapped the photo. 'But that's not the really interesting bit. See, the boy noticed the knife looked rusty, but it was in good condition otherwise, good quality. He took it home, planning to clean it up, but well, he forgot about it, got distracted. Then, two days ago, his mother found it while tidying his room, showed her husband, thinking it was junk. Fortunately his dad, ex-army man, knew better. It wasn't rust on the knife...' Anita raised her eyebrows at June as if in question.

June had gone completely still. Her face white as a sheet.

'It was actually old blood. So, the father brought the knife in to the station at Kingsbridge. Thanks to your sister's lawyer keeping up the questioning over the white car, he'd seen reference to the murder in Torcross only recently. Better to be safe than sorry, he thought. We ran forensics. The results came in today.' Anita paused, 'Is there anything you want to tell us about the knife, Ms Lane?'

June didn't move. Her eyes had gone far away. The only movement of her body was the silent bob of her throat.

Casually, Anita continued, 'You know, it's a common misconception that blood will just wash away. It doesn't. In fact, did you know that metal, like the knife blade, actually takes on blood really well? Better than most other surfaces.'

Enough. Robert leaned forward. 'Ms Lane, June, forensics found traces of Grant Huxley's blood on the knife,' he said, 'and your blood.' He paused.

'But not Eloise's.'

He stopped, eyes fixed on June. Still she didn't move. She stared off into space.

'June,' he prompted. 'We need you to tell us how this knife, with your blood and Grant Huxley's blood on it, came to be in Torcross.'

Slowly, very slowly her eyes moved down to the photo. She started shaking, pressed her eyes closed and breathed out heavily. 'It's not,' she began, choked and swallowed, pushed on, 'It's not what you think.' Her voice was tight, rough.

Robert pushed a plastic cup of water across the table to her. She flicked her eyes to him then took the cup and sipped. Working moisture back into her mouth.

'Talk us through what it is then, June,' he said.

She stared at him, eyes panicked. But she nodded.

'So, after I dropped the car off... no. No, I have to go back a bit further than that. I woke up agitated that morning. Worrying about Eloise and Jacob and Grant's plan to take my nephew away. And then I saw the knife...'

June had been in a funk all day. No matter what she did: dishes, dusting, a mini yoga flow in front of her laptop, reading to Jacob, nothing helped relieve the tension that was tracing lines of fire across her shoulders. She'd felt like this all week. Ever since Grant's letter arrived. It wasn't so much his desire for Jacob that upset her, but the flagrant betrayal. And not just of Eloise... She shook her head. She had no right to feel let down. After all, she was the one having an affair with her sister's husband. Guilt, hot and veiny, burst up from her belly and filled her chest.

For weeks now she had been seeing him, secretly, every Thursday. Living her week in a miasma of self loathing then, for a few blessed hours, enveloping herself in him. His taste, his touch, his scent. She had planned to end it for weeks. But every time she went to say it, the words dried up. She just couldn't cut herself free of him. Eloise, her dear sweet sister had no idea. She thought he wanted her back. But he was just the same cad he'd always been.

And now, he was going to take the baby.

Her phone alarm sounded, 3:45 p.m. Time to head to Salcombe. Flustered she raced from her home office, calling to Eloise as she strode through the lounge searching for her bag and keys.

'I'm off Eloise. Taking the car to the garage. I'll be home for dinner though.'

Bag located she rummaged her hands through its interior. No keys. 'Shit,' she breathed, eyes scanning wildly. She pulled a few cushions from the lounge. No joy. Racing to the kitchen she looked over the benches and even checked the fridge; Eloise wasn't the only one who could be absent-minded sometimes. The lack of sleep from caring for Jacob, she presumed. Frustrated, she opened her mouth to call again to Eloise, ask if she had seen her keys, when she spied them sitting innocently on the dining table, by the vase of dried flowers. She stalked over and scooped them up. Stopped in surprise.

There on the table, on the other side of the vase, lay her dad's old fishing knife. June frowned. Eloise must have been using it to cut the flower stems. *Silly girl*, she thought. *Even more forgetful than me.* She snatched up the knife. *Dangerous*, she worried. Jacob was starting to pull himself up on things. Little, pudgy reaching fingers searching for trouble. She'd have a word with Eloise about it. But not now. No time.

She turned for the kitchen, intending to place the knife safely in a drawer, secured by a baby-safe seal, when Eloise appeared in the room.

'Ok, lasagne sound good?' she asked.

June looked over at her sister; beautiful, fragile, vulnerable. Her throat constricted. Shame sat hot and heavy on her chest. Eloise had been so happy lately. She didn't deserve this. Any of this.

She dropped her hand below the table, hiding the knife. Not the time for a confrontation, not when June felt so damn guilty.

Eloise breezed across the room and took June by the shoulders.

'I know it's your favourite,' she smiled.

June's forehead creased in confusion. 'Sorry?'

'lasagne. I'm going to make grandma's recipe.'

'Oh, no need Lou. We have microwave ones in the freezer.'

'No,' Eloise chided, 'I am making a proper lasagne for you.' She smiled, turned and started back towards her room. Then stopped and faced June. 'You do so much for me, June. I don't know where I'd be without you. Where Jacob would be. I can't repay you, not properly. But I can do this. Ok?'

The guilt cooled, seeping down into June's gut, turning leaden and solid, a rock of self loathing in her bowel.

'You owe me nothing,' she said. 'But lasagne would be nice.'

Eloise smiled. 'See you later then.' She left the room.

June felt her body slump. 'You selfish piece of shit,' she breathed to herself. *Poor innocent Lou.*

She glanced down at the knife in her hand. *She doesn't deserve this. She doesn't. I have to stop it. I will stop it.*

She gripped the knife firmly, an idea forming in her mind.

'Should be ready by lunch tomorrow. But I'll give you a call. Ok June?'

June turned sharply, 'Oh, yep, cheers Gary,' she stammered.

'You ok, June?' Gary, short and broad of shoulder, had been her mechanic for over 20 years. You could call their association the longest male relationship in her life. Aside from her father. June surpassed a snort of derision and shook off the silly thought. She'd been miles away.

'Yes, yes I'm fine Gary. Sorry, it's been a big day.'

'Well, you do a lot June. Don't forget to take some time for you too. Ok?'

'Thanks Gary. See you tomorrow.'

Gary waved a grease-stained hand and lumbered back into the garage.

Out on the street June started for the bus stop. Then stopped. Reaching into her purse she pulled out her mobile phone and dialled a number she never thought she'd dial again.

The bus would take too long.

Ensconced in Helene's car, June sped through the narrow roads of Devon, heart pounding in her chest. It was just past 5 p.m. Grant would be at the hotel by now. Eloise was expecting her to take the bus, so she had a little over a hour of time to execute her plan. Her plan to stop Grant from destroying Eloise's world. She glanced at her handbag, swallowed against the lump of fear that surged up into her throat when she thought of the knife within and what she was going to do with it. Her mouth went dry.

The loud blare of a truck horn brought her back into the moment. She looked up and swerved quickly into a hedgerow passing bay. The truck cruised passed, driver lazily giving her the two-fingered salute. Reverse V Sign, an insult. Anger surged up through June, melting away the guilt and apprehension, replacing it with furious fire.

Fucking men! She thought violently. *Always think they can have their way. Fucking Grant fucking Huxley!*

Not this time, she resolved.

June pulled the little white Kia into the car park at Beesands. The sun had all but set, casting the beach in an orange-tinged darkness. Purse on her lap she reached inside and gripped the fishing knife. Her hands were shaking, her breathing short and shallow. She pressed her eyes together. 'For Eloise,' she said and left the car.

The hotel staff were busy in the restaurant, so June slipped in unnoticed. Slowly she crept up the hotel stairs, heading for Grant's room. She came to his closed door. This time she didn't knock.

Pulling the knife from her purse she held it by her side and swung the door open…

…and nearly screamed.

On the floor before her lay Grant in a pool of blood. June dropped the knife in shock, hands covering her mouth, as if they could hold in her terror.

She paced across the room, falling to her knees before her lover. 'Oh no,' she breathed, taking in the blood, the gash across his throat.

Grant's eyes fluttered once.

Alive? she thought, hope surging within her

She grabbed his wrist and felt for a pulse. There, faint. Frantic, she clasped her hands around the jagged slice that had severed his jugular. Blood, hot and slick, pumped out over her hands. Wildly, she scanned his body. More wounds, all over his chest, his stomach. She reached one hand down to press over the wound closest to his heart, then another at his gut. *So many.*

'Help,' she tried to call, but her throat had closed over. 'Help,' only a strained whisper escaped her lips.

Grant's eyes fluttered again, then he went limp beneath her clutching fingers.

'No,' she breathed. 'No.'

She reached into her pocket for her mobile. It slid from her grip, landing softly on the carpeted floor. She snatched it up, wiping her hand on her shirt to try and clear off enough blood to type.

Then she saw them. Laying on the floor just by Grant's still warm body. Eloise's crafting scissors.

June went cold. Froze.

'Oh god,' she whispered. 'Oh my god.'

She surged up, stepping over Grant's now lifeless body and grabbed the scissors. Her hands were shaking violently now. Everything stopped. Like someone had paused time. She stared at the scissors. Somewhere, just outside of her mind, someone was saying something, something important, logical. But June couldn't hear it. There was just the scissors, the blood, Grant. The voice came again, more insistent.

Then. *Move!*

Her limbs suddenly animated, shocked into life. She shoved the scissors into her jacket pocket, wiping her hands quickly over her shirt before zipping up the front. Shaking she stepped back over Grant's body. Her stomach roiled. *No*, she told herself firmly, fighting back the bile. She pressed her hand to her mouth and paused. Breathing slowly, trying to regain control. She rushed for the door, reaching down as she passed to take up the fishing knife she'd dropped at the door. Her thumb snagged on the sharp blade. She hissed, stuffing her thumb in her mouth and sucking up the blood.

Then she walked.

Out the door, down the stairs and into the dark winter evening.

It was pitch black by the time June pulled up at the beach car park in Torcross. Muscles trembling, she pulled hard on the hand brake and killed the engine. For a moment she didn't move. Just sat, hands on the steering wheel, eyes staring forward, unseeing.

Move.

She reached over and grabbed the knife and scissors, her handbag and climbed out of the car. Blood stains presumably from her bloodied hands, caught the car light, shining bright and red across the upholstery of the car's interior. *Tomorrow's problem*, she thought, *first things first.*

She set off towards home, pacing fast around the rim of Torcross Lake.

The air was thick with coming rain, the wind whipped fast about her body. Night, black and deep, surrounded her, shrouding her passage in darkness. She strode past her street, continuing around the lake until she reached the far end, then she turned in. Clutching the knife in one hand, the scissors in the other, she tramped through the thick overgrown brush heading for the lakeside.

The moon was a thin sliver above her, offering little light. The clouds thick and dark blocked the stars. The first drops of rain began to fall. Soon it would pour.

June held up her hands, ready to heave the two blades into the lake. Then she paused. Detectives always found weapons in lakes and streams. No, this was a bad idea. A panicked idea. She turned briskly, intending to head back home but she caught her foot on a large root in the undergrowth. Crashing down, she tried to brace her fall, but the knife and scissors hampered her. Bracken and wood tore across her wrists. She hit the ground. Smarting from the pain she surged back up. Went to continue. But her left hand was empty. She'd dropped the knife. Shoving the scissors into the loop of her belt, she began frantically feeling through the overgrowth. The dark night offered no help. The rain was falling faster now. Shaking, she grabbed her phone, swiped on the torch function and started sweeping the light through the brush. 'Come on, come on,' she hissed, eyes scanning. But she couldn't see anything.

Thunder cracked overhead, and lightning split the sky. The heavens opened.

Out of time.

Resolving to come back tomorrow, after she'd dealt with the car, June pulled up her hood against the downpour and raced out from the overgrowth. Pacing quickly back to her street and home.

'From there it's just like I said originally. I saw blood on the door frame. I rushed in, calling for Eloise. I was worried, panicked. Where was Jacob? Was he safe? Then I realised I was dripping rain water and blood all over the floor. I striped off the jacket and threw it on the dining table. I could hear Eloise singing nursery rhymes: 'three blind mice, three blind mice'. I raced into Jacob's room and found them both there. Unharmed.'

She stopped, eyes searching Robert's face. Realisation dawning across her features. There was no ally there, not anymore. She looked to Anita.

'It's the truth!' she insisted. 'I didn't tell you before because, well because who would believe me? But, but you found the knife... This time I am telling you everything that happened. I swear it. That's the story, the whole story.'

Robert sat still. Closed his eyes a moment. Heavy with his own realisation. June was going to prison.

'Ms Lane. You have lied to us every time you have given a statement. Why would we believe you now?' Anita said.

June whipped her head back to Robert, eyes pleading. 'Because,' she stammered, 'because it's the truth. This time. It is. The whole, whole truth. It's what happened. The next day I took Helene's car to the drive through in Knightsbridge and cleaned it up. And I searched, searched for that knife, every day I took Jacob for a walk around the lake to look, but I couldn't find it...'

'Ms Lane,' Anita interrupted. 'You admit to taking a knife to Grant Huxley's hotel. That you were angry and going to 'stop him."

'Stop him, yes! Threaten him. Make him leave Jacob and Eloise alone. Not kill him!'

'Are you sure of that?' Robert breathed across the table. He looked into June's face.

She stared at him, silent.

'When you borrowed her car, Ms Swifter says you told her "he was doing it again" in reference to Grant. Can you tell me what you meant by that?'

June drew back, head shaking. 'I, I don't remember...'

'Shall I tell you what I think, June?' Anita chimed in, 'I think you were desperate to stop Grant from taking Jacob away from you. We saw how close you are to the child...'

'He is my nephew! Of course I'm close to him.'

'... And you couldn't face the thought of losing another baby because of Grant.'

June's jaw dropped. It was as if the world suddenly stopped around her, like she was caught in a void.

'We know about the abortion, June,' Robert said, grim. 'What Grant did to you. And now, he was planning to take Jacob away too. So you were angry. It's understandable, natural even. Wracked with guilt. Afraid to lose Jacob, you had to do something. By your own testimony you left the house with a knife and a plan to visit Grant. Later that night he was found dead.'

'But...'

'The knife only has your blood on it, not Eloise's.'

'I explained that...'

'Forensics say the attack was frenzied. That the use of two weapons is highly probable.'

'No...'

'You are the stronger sister, Ms Lane. And Grant was not a small man. And June, you had a motive.'

'So did Eloise! Jacob is her son.'

'Eloise didn't know about the custody application.'

'She did. I told you, the letter had been moved.'

'Originally you said she hadn't seen it, then you changed your testimony. And her finger prints are not on the letter. Yours are.'

June's mouth opened and closed like a goldfish, a tight whine coming from low in her throat. Weight settled over Robert. He'd been wrong. So, so wrong.

'The reason Eloise can't remember killing Grant Huxley, is because she didn't do it, did she June? She didn't even know that Grant would be in Beesands that night. She just went for a walk.'

'No.'

'I suggest to you, Ms Lane, that on the night of 15 November, driven by your fear of losing Jacob and your own guilt over your affair with your sister's husband, you left the house with both Eloise's crafting scissors and the fishing knife with the intent to murder Grant Huxley and frame your sister for the murder.'

June's head was shaking violently side to side, her eyes filling with tears.

'This action assured Jacob would remain in your care, and the fortnightly payments by the Huxleys would continue to come in, to you.'

Glistening cheeks, face mortified, hand clamped over her mouth in horror.

'Ms June Lane,' Anita's voice crisp and clear, 'I'm charging you with the murder of Mr Grant Huxley...'

'No,' June breathed. 'No, I didn't kill him. I didn't do it. I just wanted to protect my sister. No, Robert! Please!'

Robert turned away, closing his ears to her cries of innocence. Anita finished the recording and June was taken away. Robert didn't move.

He didn't know what made him feel worse: that he'd trusted the wrong sister, or that he'd overlooked the inconsistency in the evidence regarding the jacket. The doubt was there, right from the first day, reason to at least further interrogate June. And he missed it. But Harriet, she hadn't stopped looking. She had been thorough. Even without the knife...

'Want me to call Stephanie?' Anita asked.

Robert looked up sharply, he'd been miles away.

'No, I'll do it,' he said. 'But thank you.'

Anita smiled down at him, pity writ across her features.

'It's a win, mate,' she said. 'We've finally got the right one.'

'Yeah,' Robert said. 'Yeah, it is.'

25: Absolution

'They arrested June?' Eloise's eyes widened in honest shock. 'But she...
I..., oh God! Where is Jacob?' A hand flew to her mouth, her body
tensing as if to rise in action.

Swiftly Harriet spoke, 'Jacob is safe, Eloise. Family Services placed
him with your parents. I give you my word, he is safe.'

Eloise nodded and gulped down the emotion that had constricted
her throat. Harriet waited patiently, watching as Eloise's initial fear for
her son was replaced by the understanding of what Harriet had just
told her.

The tears that had threatened from the moment Harriet started
talking spilled down Eloise's face.

'You mean, I didn't do it?' She stared at Eloise, blue eyes wide and
hopeful. 'I really didn't do it?'

Pity flooded through Harriet. Swiftly it hardened to anger at the
grave injustice Eloise had endured. So graceful, so gentle, so wronged.
She reached across the table and took Eloise's hand in hers.

'No, Eloise, you did not kill Grant Huxley.'

Choking up from deep in her throat, Eloise let out a sob. Fresh tears
coursed down her cheeks as she gripped Harriet's hand tight as
though her life depended on it. Perhaps it had.

'Thank you,' she whispered softly. 'No one else believed... I didn't
even believe. Thank you, Harriet.'

Their eyes met. Affection, raw and deep, flooded Harriet's heart.
This woman, this beautiful woman, she would go free. Justice would
be done. Finally. Harriet couldn't give back the months of freedom
Eloise had lost, the weeks in The Orchard, away from her son, missing
his first birthday. But she could give her the peace of the truth. And her
future. The anger at the injustice that had overwhelmed her emotions

cooled with the realisation. Eloise had a future now. Long and open and free.

Eloise squeezed Harriet's hand and withdrew her own. Wiping the tears from her face, she sniffed and gathered herself together. Shortly she sat up straight before Harriet, more or less composed.

'And they are sure it was June? I mean, they got it wrong with me...'

'It was June,' Harriet confirmed. 'The second weapon proves it. And the inconsistencies and lies in her testimony.'

Eloise was shaking her head. 'She always protected me,' she said. 'Would do anything to make sure I was safe... But this? To take a life for me? How could she?'

A heavy frown pulled down Harriet's brows. Had she really protected her sister? Or had she tormented her, exploited her vulnerability for her own ends.

'I'm not so sure it was for you at all,' she said.

Genuine surprise flitted across Eloise's face. 'But she's my sister. Why else would she do something so terrible?'

Harriet paused, deciding. Eloise had to know sometime, it was all going to come out now anyway. Steeling herself against the hurt she was about to inflict, she plunged into the truth. 'June terminated a pregnancy during her final year at Exeter University. It was Grant's. He left her just after the termination.'

Eloise's mouth dropped open in shock.

'The DPP will allege she never got over the loss of the baby. Then Jacob came along and she bonded with your son,' Harriet paused, braced herself for Eloise's reaction. 'I'm sorry to be the one to tell you this, Eloise. While you and Grant were working to reconcile, he and June were having an affair,' she said gently.

'No,' Eloise breathed.

'Yes, she was betraying you. They both were. So when the custody application arrived June felt it was against her too. She took it personally. She'd already lost one child to Grant, she didn't want to lose Jacob too. So she killed him and framed you, leaving herself as the sole guardian of Jacob. It was a theory I toyed with myself, but without the knife, there just wasn't enough evidence.'

Eloise's face drained of colour. A trembling hand covered her mouth. 'Can it be true?' she said.

Harriet fixed Eloise with her eyes, 'Time will tell. But the facts fit the theory. Facts don't lie, Eloise. It's a strong case. It will play well with the jury. Will they find June guilty? I can't say. What I can say, however, is that your sister isn't the woman you thought she was.'

Eloise swallowed audibly, nodding slowly. Harriet watched Eloise absorb all she had said, sympathy swelling in her chest. Suddenly she remembered Paul Lane's explanation of why his younger daughter had been committed to a psych ward as a teenager. The conviction that June was trying to hurt her. Not so ridiculous after all... Perhaps it never was?

'Do mum and dad know?' Eloise whispered, interrupting Harriet's thoughts.

'Yes, I phoned them before coming here to you.'

Eloise was shaking her head, 'Poor mum,' she said, 'she'll be shattered. To think her daughter did such a thing.'

Harriet blinked in surprise, then suppressed a wry smile. So very Eloise, to be worried about others before herself. To think of the sorrow her mother would feel over the guilt of June as something worse than the sorrow over her own guilt.

'She will come to terms with it, Eloise. The truth is always better than lies.'

'Yes, I'm sure you are right,' she smiled weakly. 'So, what happens now?'

'Now, we wait. The Attorney General has applied for what is called 'Nolle Prosequi'. It basically means to end the trial because they have charged another with the crime and know you are innocent. Tomorrow morning you are due in court. The judge will read the evidence and assess the accuracy of the application. He will find in favour. Then you will be officially cleared and free to go.'

'To go?'

'To go home, Eloise. Home to Torcross.'

'So I don't have to stay here at The Orchard? Because of my brain?' She tapped her forehead with one finger.

'No, Eloise, you don't have to stay here, or anywhere else unless you want to. Your brain is fine. Distressed, overwhelmed, yes. But not criminally ill. You suffered a double trauma. You discovered Grant's plans to take Jacob and that triggered a fugue state, which caused you to regress into automatic. You went for your regular walk.'

'I left my baby...'

'Doctor Taylor says that is an expected reaction. You went into routine, a normal response to extreme stress. Then you suffered the even greater horror of seeing your sister covered in blood and of believing you had perpetrated such a terrible crime. I think, considering the facts, your amnesia is quite understandable. Doctor Taylor says, given these exceptional circumstances, you have done really well. After the six months of intensive treatment you have received here and the implementation of your new medication and treatment plan, he is confident you are stable enough to go home and take care of Jacob. He does recommend that you see a psychologist, though, to help you deal with all this. But you get to choose who and when and how. You are not a criminal, Eloise. You are a free citizen. Your life will be your own again.'

Eloise blew out a heavy breath. 'Okay, it's just a lot to get my head around after...' She gestured to the walls of The Orchard.

Harriet nodded, 'You will get there. And you will be with Jacob.'

Eloise smiled, lips trembling. 'Yes,' she said. 'And no one will take him from me again.'

26: Nolle Prosequi

Eloise cried. Gentle, controlled tears of relief, grief and freedom.

She was sitting in the dock of the Crown Court of Exeter. Judge Bradford had just dismissed the case against her, accepting the Prosecution's application for Nolle Prosequi. For the first time in six months, Eloise was a free woman. Harriet watched her in private awe; gentle woman, yes, but also strong. She had faced the most horrible possibility, that she was a murderer, and she had stood up. Now, she was absolved.

Behind her in the public gallery sat her parents Dorothy and Paul, faces drawn tight over their ageing bones. They looked exhausted. *A difficult day for them*, Harriet realised. The joy of a daughter freed, the sorrow of another in prison. However much seeded from parental care, hopefully they would now learn that Eloise was not one to so easily dismiss. She was ready to be her own person, outside of June's shadow and their control.

Stephanie Emmetts stood stiffly beside DS Robert Fields, both tired, defeated. Harriet felt a flash of pure righteous rage burn through her mind as Robert looked up and saw her staring at him. Shame flashed across his face. This time he was the one to quickly turn away.

In the dock Eloise was now crying freely, tears of vindication and relief flooding her cheeks.

Harriet blinked back the answering moisture that glistened threateningly along her eyelids. Their eyes met across the court room, and Eloise smiled. A light of promise.

Randell Dawes tapped Harriet's arm gently.

'Well done, Harriet,' he said.

Harriet turned from the crying Eloise and faced the QC. His old eyes shone with an unexpected light, his diminutive frame pulled up straighter than she'd ever seen. A smile hovered on his lips.

'40 years in this business,' he continued, 'I've worked every case imaginable. Tested every angle. But never, not once, have I seen the like of this. You have reminded me of one of my favourite axioms, 'do not confuse knowledge with the smell of cold stone.''

He paused, curled fingers tapped Harriet's folder of case notes.

'The facts were clear. Our defence was clear. Open and shut. An easy win, Automatism and hospitalisation. But you,' he stared at Harriet, 'you worked the facts. Took them out of the office and into the world, walked the grounds of the crime, spoke to the people of the towns. You dogged the evidence, kept up the question of the car, discovered the inconsistency with the jacket, and you didn't settle. We are here, she,' he nodded towards Eloise, now being led out of the court room, 'she is free, in large part because of you.'

Pride swelled up in Harriet. She felt her shoulders straighten, her posture lengthen. She fought back the flood of emotion, working to remain composed and professional.

Dawes gave her a knowing smile, 'If ever there was a time to express how you feel honestly, it is now,' he said gently. 'You have done a great thing here today Harriet. The full realisation of it may take a while to settle over you. Allow yourself to feel it. All of it. You are an excellent lawyer, Ms Bell. I am honoured to have worked beside you.'

It was too much. The months of self doubt, the sense that something wasn't right with the case, her belief in Eloise. And now to be proved right. To have seen justice done. Harriet glanced down, ostensibly gathering her notes and whisked a stray tear from her eye. 'Thank you,' she croaked without looking up.

Dawes patted her arm. 'Let's go. Just the final paperwork to go over with our client and then she leaves this court a free woman.'

Now composed, Harriet met his steady gaze. 'Yes, let's go. She has waited long enough.'

They were walking together down the main corridor of the Crown Court when he called to her. Harriet paused, looked to the ceiling and heaved a sigh. Dawes turned. Seeing Robert Fields approaching fast he frowned, then flicked his eyes to Harriet. 'I'll catch you up,' she said.

The aged QC paused. For a moment Harriet thought he would argue to stay, then he nodded.

'Don't be long.'

Harriet nodded gratefully and turned to face Robert.

'Thank you for stopping,' Robert began. He paused, hovering before her, uncertain.

'I wanted to say...' a swallow, he cleared his throat, 'You were right. And well done.'

Surprised, Harriet gaped a moment. She didn't know what she'd been expecting him to say. But it wasn't that.

Robert continued, 'June blindsided me. She seemed so, honest. I let myself be conned by her manner and didn't properly review the facts. It seemed so clear cut.' He paused, nodding to himself. 'You brought justice here today, Harriet. Thank you.'

Stunned, Harriet stared at Robert.

He looked exhausted. His dark eyes, normally sparkling with the promise of joy, were dull and defeated. All the words of indignation and blame that had surged to her lips at the sound of his voice, dissipated on her tongue as she took in his despondent posture, the shame on his face.

'The evidence seemed obvious,' she found herself saying, comforting. 'I think you did what any detective would have done. It's your job to investigate and charge. It's mine to raise doubt.'

He smiled ruefully, 'I'm meant to charge the *right* person, Harriet. It's about justice, remember?'

She smiled wryly, remembering their conversation on motives in the work place. It seemed a lifetime ago.

Gently, she said, 'Cut yourself a break, Robert. You work hard, we all know it. You just got this one wrong, yeah?'

'Yeah.'

'Besides, we can't all be perfect,' she quipped, offering him a sassy smile and tossing her brown locks over one shoulder.

He huffed a laugh, 'True, true.' A small grin played on his lips. His eyes lit a little. Harriet felt that familiar pull towards him, the desire to just share space with him and talk. To flirt and joke.

'I should go.'

'Of course. Harriet, thank-you,' his warm eyes held hers. Not trusting herself to speak, she nodded, feeling awkward. Neither of them moved. Both standing as if frozen on the steps of the Crown Court, caught between emotions; the challenge of now, the possibility of the future. The silence stretched between them. Harriet felt her resolve waver.

But no, not today. Too much had happened today. It was time to go.

Over Robert's shoulder Harriet spied Eloise's parents, Dorothy and

Paul, coming out of the courtroom. Dorothy's eyes caught hers and she visibly stiffened. Grateful for the excuse, Harriet's mask of professionalism snapped back up. She bid Robert a quick good day and hurried over to the Lanes.

They stopped at her approach. Paul's face was drawn, emotions pulled in, tucked safely out of view. Dorothy, on the other hand, wore open malice on her face.

'Mr and Mrs Lane,' Harriet began. 'I am glad to have this opportunity to speak with you both in person. This must be a very difficult day for you. I can't imagine what you are going through…'

'No, you can't,' Dorothy snapped, cutting Harriet off.

Harriet turned to Dorothy. The small woman was seething with a passion unlike any Harriet had ever seen in her before.

'We hired you to defend our Lou. Not convict Junie.'

'Dotty…' Paul started, laying a gentle hand on his wife's arm.

'No, Paul,' she said, 'I am going to say it.'

She rounded on Harriet, eyes fierce. 'Do you think this is what we want? One daughter jailed for life for murder and the other removed from the help she needs?'

'Mrs Lane,' Harriet began, 'Eloise is innocent. Regardless of her need for help she should not be convicted of a crime she did not commit.'

Dorothy let out vexed breath. 'You honestly believe Junie did this?' she demanded. Her eyes scanned Harriet's face.

'I am not June's lawyer. I can't speak for all the evidence in the case against her. But from what I have seen in my research to defend Eloise, it does seem so, yes. The facts fit.'

'The facts!' Dorothy exclaimed. 'The facts! What about the truth in the heart? What a mother knows? What she doesn't want to acknowledge openly, but she carries deep inside. What about the truth?'

'Mrs Lane,' Harriet said calmly, 'I understand you are upset. This is all a lot to take in. But justice was served here today. Eloise should not be incarcerated. You must see that.'

'All I see is a young lawyer who is too clever for her own good.'

'Mrs Lane…'

'No more,' Dorothy held up a hand to silence Harriet. 'I hope it was worth it,' she said, eyes boring into Harriet's.

With that she and Mr Lane walked away, leaving Harriet standing alone in shock behind them. As they reached the large front doors of the Crown Court Paul glanced back over his shoulder at Harriet, eyes filled with sorrow and shook his head softly.

Confused and upset Harriet adjusted her jacket and ran a hand over her hair to smooth it. *It's a bad day for them,* she reasoned, *nothing more.* Forcibly putting the encounter from her mind she turned back down the corridor, mind focused on her client, who was now free.

27: The wronged sister

The Crown Court loomed behind them, a bright white frame against the pale blue sky. Eloise breathed deeply, smiled. Harriet felt peace settle inside her own self. Eloise was out.

Laughing, Eloise turned to Harriet, giddy joy spreading across her face. She was clad in jeans and a pink shirt. The pink set off her beautiful eyes, lightened her complexion. She looked years younger than she had inside The Orchard. Youthful and free.

'I can never thank you enough,' Eloise enthused. 'This is all because of you.'

'No,' Harriet said, 'it is because of justice. You deserve this Eloise.'

Eloise nodded, face momentarily solemn. It was a heavy burden to hold; freedom at the expense of your sister. Harriet hoped Eloise could surmount it.

'Doctor Taylor gave you a list of recommended psychologists?'

'Yes.'

'Do ring them, Eloise. When you are ready. I think they will really help with all of this.'

'Of course,' Eloise turned away.

Harriet let the topic drop. Who was she to push? Eloise had just spent six months locked up awaiting trial for something she didn't do. She had been through untold stresses coming to terms with the murder of her husband and the belief that she was responsible. It would take time for her to be ready to trust anyone again after this.

Harriet changed the subject, 'So, what are your first plans for when you get home?'

'Cuddles with Jacob.' Eloise beamed. 'I have so missed my little man. His first birthday... He will have grown so much.' Sadness drifted across her features. So much time, lost. Harriet watched her rally, pulling herself back from the abyss of self-pity into the future of possibility. 'You'll have to come down to Torcross and meet him,' she exclaimed.

'I have met him already,' Harriet answered gently.

Eloise flicked a glance at her, eyes narrowing. 'No, you met my sister's nephew. Not my son.' She straightened her shoulders. Harriet frowned. *Odd reaction.* Yet, was it really? After all she had been through, after what her sister did to try and keep Jacob for herself...

'Oh!' Eloise suddenly turned to Harriet, 'And I must make you a new folder. A felt one, for your notes and files. Such important and amazing work you do. That dreary black one has to go. It will give me a new crafting project. Something to focus on, something positive and meaningful.'

Harriet, caught up in Eloise's gentle affection, laughed happily. She couldn't stand felt art, but it was the thought that mattered.

'Well, that would mean a lot, Eloise. Though, you'll have to wait until you get some new crafting scissors, unfortunately. Your pair will remain with evidence. You won't get them back, I'm afraid.'

Eloise waved this away, looking out to the street before them. 'Those old things? No loss there. I only ever use my scissors for crafting anyway. And they are safely tucked away in my office. Ready and waiting.'

'You have another pair of scissors?'

'Of course. You don't use the good set for dirty work, do you Harriet?'

Harriet felt her brows bunch, 'But I thought you couldn't find your scissors that night? That June had taken them.'

'Hmmm,' she hummed vaguely, gaze forward. 'Isn't it amazing how often we are underestimated, Harriet?'

Mind still focused on her previous comment and thrown by the change of topic Harriet stammered, 'I'm sorry?'

'You and I, or at least, people like us. I think it might be because we are small, we look frail,' Eloise turned to face Harriet, eyes suddenly fierce, piercing. 'People just assume things about you, your character, your power. They think you are vulnerable, that you can be controlled, pushed around. Doesn't it just make you mad? You must find it all the time in your profession! But I wasn't fooled Harriet, not for one moment. I saw your potential.'

She broke off, looking back down the street, breathing suddenly laboured. Harriet nodded warily. *I guess that's right*, Harriet thought.

Perhaps I should give myself more credit for my management of arrogant people...

'Yes, but Eloise, what were you saying about the...'

'I've had enough of living that way,' Eloise interrupted. 'More than enough.'

Eyes fixed on the horizon, she took a deep breath, 'They thought they were so secretive, so clever. But I knew about June and Grant. And I wasn't surprised. Boringly predictable really. I knew she'd never got over him. And Grant, well, my husband would fuck anything on two legs if it was willing.'

Harriet blinked in surprise at the rough language and the distain that dripped from her words.

At the revelation.

'You knew?'

Eloise had folded her arms across her chest in angry defiance.

'Grant always had another woman on the go, right from when we were first married,' Eloise said, 'I didn't mind, more time for me to be me, doing my own thing. I loved the freedom. But things changed when I got pregnant with Jacob. Grant became attentive, interested. Suddenly wanted to know what I was doing, where I was going. Telling me what I should and shouldn't do, because of the baby. It was just like being home with mum and dad. Worse... he hated it when I disagreed. Hated it!'

Eloise gave a short shake of her head, like a nervous tick, before rolling her shoulders as if releasing a store of pent up tension. Harriet had seen that gesture before, when they talked about Hollydale...

'I wanted out,' she continued, 'but I couldn't leave Grant, not if I wanted to stay in the city. There wasn't the money if I did.'

She paused, rubbing her hands on her arms, eyes far away, 'A return to being unwell was the perfect answer. You learn a thing or two about playing the system when you're committed.'

A knowing smile.

'The perfect answer?'

'My "troubles" meant mum and dad were forced to help. No lectures about "duty as a wife" and all that crap. They just paid the rent after Grant moved out, got me a nanny. But they couldn't leave it could they? Oh, no, they had to meddle!'

Eloise took a shuddering breath and ran a hand through her hair. Harriet stood staring at her, forehead creased in confusion.

'They pulled the rent, moved us down to the house on Hiddley. That fucking stupid holiday shack. Then June gave up everything to come and support me. Always was a martyr that one. "So you can relax. Enjoy each day and Jacob." I mean, how would she know what I wanted? She's never asked! The only ones who were truly helpful were the Huxleys paying us support money for Jacob, no strings attached. But me, I was back in my childhood again, under the thumb of my parents and my sister. When Grant came back I was so relieved. It was my chance to get out again.'

She shrugged, 'I was happy to play along, I wanted to be in London, and divorce didn't interest me anymore. I was sure I could make it work. Though, if I'm honest, it was a relief when he and June first started seeing each other. Took the pressure off of me. I mean, I had Jacob, why would I want any more sex with Grant? You know?'

She looked at Harriet as if in shared conspiracy. Harriet faked an agreeing nod. A strong sense of unease slowly uncoiling in her gut.

'Anyway, I thought I had it all going well. Then the letter arrived from the Family Court. Sole custody. Can you believe it? The fucking cheek of it! I wasn't having that, oh no.'

'You knew about the letter? Before you were interviewed?'

Eloise cocked her head, giving Harriet an incredulous glance.

Right, yeah, underestimating. But...

Eloise continued, 'What to do?' she mused to herself, one finger resting on her chin in a mime of thoughtfulness, 'Junie was the answer, of course.'

She looked up at Harriet, eyes two orbs of blue flame. 'No one was going to take my son. No one.'

A chill ran down Harriet's spine, she swallowed. The fury in Eloise's eyes, the depth of hate brimming there, shocked her to the core. Yet wasn't that the reaction you would expect from a mother defending her child? It was only natural. Except...

Breaking into Harriet's thoughts, Eloise went on, 'I booked the car in for a Thursday, I knew it would interrupt June's plans to visit Grant, frustrate her, especially with the secret of the custody letter hanging around her neck like a millstone. Another lie to keep inside. She never was good with guilt, our Junie. '

'You knew they met on Thursdays?' Harriet said, breath coming faster now.

Eloise didn't pause, her words flowed on ignoring Harriet's question, lost in her recollection, 'I made sure June knew just how thankful I was to her, for everything. For giving up her life in London, for taking care of me and Jacob, for being the only person in the world I could depend on, trust fully,' she laughed low and vile. 'It was quite fun really, seeing just how deeply those words cut her. When I saw she'd taken dad's old fishing knife, well...'

Shock locked Harriet's brain, her stomach clenched tight.

'Eloise,' she breathed, throat tight. Swallowing she continued, 'Are you saying that you manipulated June into killing your husband?'

'Oh!' Eloise turned two big blue eyes, wide and full of innocence, to Harriet, 'did I think that?' she looked momentarily confused and glanced away, watching the line of pine trees swaying in the gentle breeze.

A small crease marked the perfect surface of her forehead as she slowly shook her head, 'No, I don't think I truly ever thought she would, not really. You can never be sure what a person will do, can you, Harriet?' A pause. 'I needed to be sure.'

Harriet's breathing was coming in short painful bursts now, the heaviness of panic settling along her limbs. Her palms began to sweat.

'Eloise,' she began, almost panting, 'Eloise, are you saying...?'

'Hmmm?' Eloise regarded Harriet with calm sea eyes and smiled gently. 'I'm not saying anything love,' she replied, cocking her head to the side. 'It's like you said. The facts are clear. June was angry with Grant and she took the knife. Not much room for reasonable doubt there. Justice done.'

She turned away, face set with determination. Harriet couldn't speak. A dark feeling had flooded her senses. Her knees felt weak.

Eloise breathed in deeply, oblivious to Harriet's distress. 'And I can finally go home,' she said to the skies arms stretched out wide as if taking the world into her arms. 'No more digging around in confusing memories. I can hug my baby, take Bella for a walk,' she spun round to face Harriet, joy writ across her features, 'I can see a sunset! You know I haven't seen one since that night? It's always so beautiful off the coast of Beesands...'

Harriet froze.

'You remember being in Beesands?'

'It was such a cold night, I absolutely made the wrong choice of jacket.' Eloise laughed lightly, shaking her head as if in rueful recollection of a past oversight.

Harriet opened her mouth to speak, once, twice, throat tight, questions trembling through her mind, 'Eloise...' she managed.

Two blue eyes, open, sincere.

Abruptly, a car swung into the car park. Eloise looked away, 'Oh, here's my ride.'

Harriet glanced at the car, saw Helene Swift behind the wheel.

'Your parents aren't picking you up?'

'No, they have to collect Jacob from their neighbours. He's with them so they could come today. And they are very tired after all of this... fuss with June,' her eyes reflected sympathy, understanding. 'And as you know, Helene owes me. A lot of people owe me.' The fire lit for a moment, then banked.

Helene pulled up in front of them and leaned across the car to open the passenger side door. Eloise stepped over, bent down and said something quickly to Helene. Helene nodded.

Eloise turned back to Harriet. 'Thank you again Harriet,' she smiled softly, 'I could never have done it all without you.'

A glimmer, cold and foreign, shone from her eyes and was gone, replaced with the open innocence Harriet was used to.

'I'll send you that felt folder as soon as I can. And remember, it's a good thing to be underestimated. An advantage. Took me years to realise that, it's really a strength. Bye for now!'

She settled into the car, drawing her seatbelt across her chest as Helene pulled away from the curb leaving Harriet standing alone, armpits slick with sweat. Mind numb with shock.

'Fuck,' she breathed, hands shaking. She took a deep breath and squeezed her eyes shut. Her body felt frozen despite the gentle warmth of the spring sun.

Suddenly, Harriet burst into action, striding for her car at a brisk place. She had to move, had to get away. She needed to think.

The morning light filtered softly through the curtains of Harriet's lounge room. Her hands cradled a cup of coffee, long gone cold. Dressed in yesterday's suit, blanket wrapped about her shoulders, Harriet stared, unseeing, at a dent on her coffee table.

She'd come straight back to her apartment after accompanying Eloise as she was released from the Orchard, messaged her secretary that she was working from home, and slumped down on her couch.

She hadn't moved since. The long dark hours of night spent tossing and turning, mind in turmoil.

Free from the Orchard, Eloise had transformed, seemingly before Harriet's very eyes, anger, bitterness, determination had emanated from her. Yet wasn't that to be expected? The natural response to all she had been through: the betrayal of her husband and sister, the fear of losing her child. Breaking free from a lifetime of control from her parents.

But her words could suggest more, much more…

She'd admitted knowledge she previously denied. Details of the night of Grant's death. Was her memory returning, or had she never lost it? And what did those memories mean now?

Harriet pressed her palm against her forehead, fighting the wave of nausea that threatened to empty her stomach. Placing her cold mug on the table, she reached for her phone, bringing up Robert's number as she had done several times already that morning. She needed a sounding board, someone else to talk it all through with. Together they could make sense of it all.

Robert. He'd believed Eloise was guilty, right from the start. Harriet's instincts said the opposite. Had he been right all along?

She paused, thumb hovering over the call button. She couldn't make the call. What held her back? Pride? Uncertainty?

Harriet's stomach cramped, the nervous fluttering intensifying. She curled up on her side, pulling the blanket tight about her shoulders. Seeking warmth, comfort.

She felt unanchored, cut loose, lost.

Old versus new crafting scissors. Did the whole case really come down to those few little words? The clue to the truth, or just a throw away sentence?

Picking the sleep from her eyes before vigorously rubbing her face in an effort to work some feeling back into her skin, Harriet ordered herself to focus. She needed to think clearly, logically. Review the facts. Her eyes stared blankly at the white ceiling.

What had Eloise said, really? That she had manipulated June, definitely. But to what end? To feel guilt over her betrayal and confront Grant on Eloise's behalf? Or to commit murder? Did it even matter? June chose to take the knife of her own free will…

But was it really June who killed Grant? Or had Eloise got there first, cold wind at her back, old scissors in hand, filled with rage at Grant's betrayal and the threat of losing her son?

She'd said just enough to raise doubt but not enough to form a conclusion. Leaving Harriet with clues and suggestions, but no hard evidence, nothing she could use to confirm or deny this question that now wracked her soul; impotent in the face of potential injustice.

And what she had said about them being similar. Eloise's fury at being underestimated was too close to her own anger at her father's dismissal of her career, her rage at Robert's dishonesty...

A defiant spark lit inside her, it wasn't Harriet who had decided to arrest and charge June Lane, that was on the DPP. All she'd done was defend her client, create doubt. That was her job wasn't it? Defence. If the DPP couldn't get their act together that was on them.

Harriet groaned.

No.

No matter how hard she tried to make herself believe that, she couldn't.

Everyone deserved a defence, that was her calling, the whole reason she'd entered the law in the first place. But after Eloise, that just wasn't enough anymore. She found something real to defend, a true injustice to fight against. She'd trusted the system. Evidence, facts, truth. But had she just been the one to corrupt it? Had she saved a vulnerable, innocent woman from unjust incarceration? Or had she allowed a manipulative psychopath to turn her head and set a killer free?

The knowledge that she could have been terribly wrong sat heavily on her chest. Filled with this doubt, how could she stand before a judge and argue confidently for a client?

Harriet stood up suddenly, limbs shaking in silent rage. 'No,' she shouted to the empty apartment. 'Stop this self pity. You are better than this!'

Determined, she strode for the bathroom, pulling her clothes from her body as she went. Eloise had rocked her to her core, made her doubt the very essence of herself as a lawyer. But Harriet was not so easily beaten. She might be powerless to act on her doubts over the Huxley murder, that was in the hands of the DPP now. She had to trust the process.

Regardless, she was still a lawyer, and a fine one at that. And she would see justice done.

Turning on the shower she stepped beneath the jets, the shock of the ice cold water clearing away a night spent in the agony of self doubt. *Enough wallowing*, she told herself firmly. It was time to get back to work. Time to step up.

Towelling herself dry she selected a fresh coal black suit and four inch heels with red soles. Hair neatly pulled back in a bun at her nape, Harriet stood straight and gazed at herself in the mirror. Strong, professional, unwavering. She was ready. There were cases to see to.

Yet just below the surface the doubt still shimmered, and the unanswered question remained: which sister really killed Grant Huxley?

Prologue

The little girls stood on the sandy pebbles of Torcross beach. One tall in the awkward way of bourgeoning adolescence, one plump with childhood. Both blonde and fair.

On the sand at their backs lounged their parents, reclining elegantly beneath a beach umbrella striped green and red, forming a wall of dazzling colour as it blended with the other umbrellas that lined the seaside. Father dozing, mother's nose in a book. Above them the sun shone strong and hot, warming the holidaymakers, the sand and the sea.

The smaller girl, clad in a pink and frilly swimsuit, clutched a pebble in her short, fat fingers.

'Now, turn it like this,' said the tall one, gently taking the small hand and helping the fingers to adjust around the smooth, cream stone. 'Then throw!'

She demonstrated skilfully, her pebble skimming across the calm waters of the bay and bouncing.

'1, 2, 3, 4, wahoo! Best one today,' she exclaimed, clapping.

The pudgy pink girl frowned grumpily.

'Ok sweetie, your turn.'

The little girl took up her stone and… it plopped into the water, heavy and flat. She stamped a little foot into the sand in anger, arms crossed in the tiny fury of childhood failure, and a good dose of petulance.

'Hey, don't be upset, Lou. It takes practice, that's all. Come on, grumpy, let's take a break and swim!'

In an unmistakeable display of dominance, the older girl clapped the younger on the back, hard, then streaked into the blue waters, all angles and lines and green bathers. She stroked out a little way then lay back in the water, floating peacefully.

SPLASH!

The girl reared up as the wash of the rock plunging into the sea splattered over her face.

'Hey, careful!' she called, 'Aim out that way.' She pointed down the beach before returning to her gentle floating.

On the sand the little face glowered at her sister. Chubby fingers closed around a new stone. Heavy, dark, round, not flat and smooth. Carefully, she balled her fist about it, just as her father had showed her to grip a cricket ball. Eyes focused forward, she brought up her soft fleshed arm and took aim.

This time she would not miss.

Printed in Great Britain
by Amazon